Alexandra popped into his thoughts constantly. And now she seemed to eye him carefully, as if weighing whether to wade into dangerous waters.

"Are you as hard on your son as you are on yourself?" she asked.

He frowned and searched his recent memory. "No, I'm not. I know he's grieving and acting out because of it. I appreciate your kindness and all you've done for him. So, can we effect a truce between us?"

She looked down and flicked at a splatter of mud on her thigh. When she looked back up, the sun sparkled in her eyes.

"A truce would be good," she said.

He reached out to shake her hand, thinking to seal the deal, but it felt as if he might have sealed his fate instead. Because the feel of her small, soft hand sliding into his short-circuited whatever was left of his brain.

Books by Kate Welsh

Love Inspired

KATE WELSH

is a two-time winner of Romance Writers of America's coveted Golden Heart® Award and a finalist for RWA's RITA® Award in 1999. Kate lives in Havertown, Pennsylvania, with her husband of over thirty years. When not at work in her home office, creating stories and the characters that populate them, Kate fills her time in other creative outlets. There are few crafts she hasn't tried at least once, or a sewing project that hasn't been a delicious temptation. Those ideas she can't resist grace her home or those of friends and family.

As a child she often lost herself in creating make-believe worlds and happily-ever-after tales. Kate turned back to creating happy endings when her husband challenged her to write down the stories in her head. With Jesus so much a part of her life, Kate found it natural to incorporate Him into her writing. Her goal is to entertain her readers with wholesome stories of the love between two people the Lord has brought together and to teach His truth while she entertains.

ABIDING LOVE

KATE WELSH

Love Inspired

Published by Steeple Hill Books™

STEEPLE HILL BOOKS

Steeple
Hill®

ISBN 0-373-87262-3

ABIDING LOVE

Copyright © 2004 by Kate Welsh

This edition published by arrangement with Steeple Hill Books.

® and TM are trademarks of Steeple Hill Books, used under license. Trademarks indicated with ® are registered in the United States Patent and Trademark Office, the Canadian Trade Marks Office and in other countries.

www.SteepleHill.com

Printed in U.S.A.

Therefore, if anyone is in Christ, he is a new creation; old things have passed away; behold, all things have become new.

—*2 Corinthians* 5:17

For Bobbie.
Thanks for all the long talks
and caring concern through the years,
your cha-chink comments that bring such clarity
to situations and mostly the laughs. You enrich
my life and writing with your friendship.

Prologue

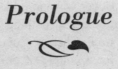

"This is it, Xandra, old girl. 245 Hollow Stump Lane," Alexandra whispered hoarsely into the still, fall night. She wasn't old, of course. Just thirty-two. But she felt twice that as she stood in the moonlight-dappled shadow of a huge oak tree, tired to the bone.

Sighing, she leaned against the tree, chilled by the fall freeze, her light denim jacket affording little protection from the wind. She gazed up at the house she'd walked miles to reach. The lights were on inside the big old stone Victorian. All and all, it looked like a nice place to live. It looked safe.

Safe.

Maybe her long journey home was over.

"We tend to call the police when we find someone skulking around in the dark," a disembodied female voice said from the top of the porch steps.

Xandra closed her eyes, fighting tears. She knew that voice. Did she live under a dark star? How could the one woman who could help her turn out to be the one woman in the world with the most reason to laugh in her face? The sad thing was, because she'd let herself be such a coward all these years, she knew she deserved no better.

Swinging her nearly empty backpack onto her shoulder, Xandra stepped out into the light of the full moon. Elizabeth Boyer was more likely to spit on her than help her, but she had nothing left to lose. She was on foot in rural Chester County. Her pockets were empty but for a couple of dollars and change. She wore thrift store clothes and used sneakers. She'd slept in homeless shelters, on buses, in train stations for months. And Michael had beaten and frightened any Lexington pride out of her a year before that.

"A woman gave me this address. This is New Life Inn, isn't it?"

"Alexandra Lexington?"

The disbelief in Elizabeth's voice wasn't new to Xandra. She'd heard that same disbelief in the voices of the police officers back in California who'd responded to her 911 calls. Most recently she'd heard it from her own mother when she'd shown up at her childhood home a few hours ago, only to be turned away.

Michael Balfour was a saint—a blameless saint— according to her mother and the rest of the world. Her husband was frantic, she'd told Xandra. He had been for the months it had taken her to make her way home to Pennsylvania. He'd spent a fortune on detectives trying to find her. Oh, and Xandra was apparently "delusional" now. She needed to go back home. Michael would get her the help she seemed to need. They would book the flight back to the prison of her husband's Northern California vineyard. But no. They couldn't, in good conscience, help her in any other way. After all, Michael would never forgive them if they made it too easy for her to remain apart from him.

"Alexandra Lexington Balfour, actually," she admitted now to Elizabeth. And it *was* an admission. Both her surnames brought her only shame before this courageous woman.

"I can't believe you'd come here," Elizabeth snapped. "Hasn't your family punished me enough for something that wasn't my fault? The women living here deserve peace. Take potshots at me in public all you want, but leave New Life Inn out of it."

"Causing you one more minute of undeserved pain is the last thing I want," Xandra said quietly. "Elizabeth, please. The only reason I'm here is for help, just like those women inside. And I need help for the same reason they do." She hated that her voice shook with exhaustion. With desperation. With fear. "I've walked at least ten miles today, and I'm not sure I can get all the way back to town again. I'm just about out of cash. I'm two dollars and twenty-seven cents from having no options at all."

Elizabeth's turnaround was instantaneous. "Of course we'll help you, Alexandra," she said, rushing down the steps, nothing but kindness in her tone now.

Xandra's rubbery legs just about went liquid beneath her and she lost her long-fought battle with tears. When she'd boarded a bus at dawn two months earlier in the small Northern California town of Summit Falls, she had sworn she'd shed her last tear over Michael Balfour.

"I'm not crying over him," she told Elizabeth, who was now supporting her with an arm around her waist. "It's just that I thought they'd side with me this time."

"Who?"

"My parents."

Elizabeth sighed. "We certainly hit the jackpot when parents were assigned, didn't we?"

Xandra huffed out a breath and stared into the kind eyes of Elizabeth Boyer. "You should have pressed charges against Jason. My brother deserved to go to prison for rape. He was a mean and violent boy who grew into a monster. I'm sorry for what he did to you. I'm sorry for what *we* did afterward."

Elizabeth tilted her head, her long blond hair shimmering in the moonlight. "If I remember every nasty encounter correctly over the years, you always stayed silent. I saw you as your mother's supporter, but you were really just standing there, right?"

"Sometimes silence isn't always golden. I found that out the hard way in a town my husband—" Xandra closed her eyes, shook her head and corrected herself. They were the hardest words she would ever speak but she forced herself to say them aloud to Elizabeth. "No…my abuser. In the town my *abuser* owned."

Elizabeth smiled kindly. "You're going to be fine, Alexandra. You've already taken several very important steps that take a lot of women too many years to make. Welcome to a new life."

Chapter One

"I still don't see why I had to come," sixteen-year-old Mark Boyer groused to his father.

Adam Boyer stopped, turned back and faced his son right where they stood, in the middle of the Tabernacle's parking lot. He was nervous himself, so he knew how the kid felt. Mark had never met his father's side of the family. Adam's parents had cut all ties to him because he chose Annapolis and a Navy career over Princeton and what they saw as a socially acceptable and lucrative profession.

Adam sighed, striving for the right amount of reassurance and authority. He wished he was better at this full-time parenting stuff. As he looked at his confused son, the familiar anger at his ex-wife—late ex-wife—rose to choke him once again. "It's your aunt's wedding," he told Mark, trying not to grit his teeth as he explained for what seemed like the hundredth time.

"I didn't want to move here and I don't need another aunt. I have one," Mark shot back as he slouched along, his hands stuffed in his jacket pockets, his broadening shoulders hunched against the unfamiliar cold of the Pennsylvania winter. "An aunt I wanted to live with. This aunt sounds so lame. Getting married on Valentine's Day. Pul-eeze. And, unless I'm totally off, that church we're headed for is a barn!"

Adam glanced at the building. It was indeed a barn that had been cleverly converted into a church. So his sister had turned out to be a little offbeat. At least this meant she wasn't as snobbish as he'd always feared she would become under the tutelage of their class-conscious parent. Her letters showed that and more. Beth was what she called a committed Christian. Her letters were full of God and her love for Him.

"I don't think God cares where people worship, son. So why should we? Jesus was born in a stable. I imagine He still listens to people praying from one. I think this means your aunt's a lot of fun."

"I don't care. I wanted to live with Aunt Sky."

Adam sighed. "And I've told you, I have nothing against your aunt Skyler. She's your mother's sister, but I'm your father. We'll continue to see her, but I'm not handing you over to her, and I'm sure not marrying her to please you. Or her. I loved your mother. But our marriage ended a long time ago. I accepted that she fell in love with Jerry and I moved on with my life.'' A tiny fib, but that was his own private pain.

''But you married mom and you said you loved her and Aunt Sky is practically Mom's carbon copy.''

Adam sighed. ''No one is someone else's carbon copy, Mark. And I don't want a carbon copy of your mom in any case. That wouldn't be fair to either Skyler or me to try recapturing a past long gone, with her as a stand-in. Got it?''

Mark shot him a belligerent look.

''Can't you just relax and give this a shot? I want to get to know Beth again. I've missed most of her life. I didn't think she'd ever want to see me again, until I got her letter just before I was deployed. Is it so much to ask that you try, or at least pretend, to have a nice time, just for today? I'm supposed to be inside the church before she arrives, or it'll ruin the surprise. And we did go to a lot of trouble to make this a surprise. We have to get a move on.'' Adam turned and started toward the front doors of the building.

''Yeah. Sure. If you ask me, this whole thing is more trouble than it's worth. But who asks me about anything? You moved us into a house that looks like a mausoleum and her church is a barn. How lame is this?'' Mark grumbled again as he fell into step.

It appeared Mark's word of the day was *lame*. Adam closed his eyes for a second and sighed. Wasn't life supposed to get easier?

Adam understood some of what Mark was feeling. No one had asked either of them if they wanted their lives disrupted. The only difference was that Adam, as an adult, had more control. But with that control came the awesome responsibility for someone else's happiness. So he bit his tongue and clapped Mark on the shoulder, saying, "Come on, pal. Lighten up. Think of the stories you can tell your friends about your weird Pennsylvania relatives when you talk to them."

Adam glanced around as they approached the building, following Mark's gaze. They were certainly in Pennsylvania. Snow covered the ground and roofs, but the walkways and parking lot had been scraped clean and had dried in the winter sunshine. The crisp air tickled his nose. Even after all these years it felt like home.

Having lived in Southern California for most of his adult life, he'd forgotten peaceful winter days like this even existed. He'd been deployed all over the world at different times, and often those hot spots were in pretty cold places, but life on an operation was a world apart from the everyday world he was living in now.

Inside the church, they found a bustle of activity. A man about his own age stood just inside the door.

"Please tell me you're Elizabeth's brother," the guy said, sounding more than a little anxious.

The groom? He wasn't dressed like one, but then this *had* been a barn.

Adam figured his Navy uniform was a dead give-away. "Adam Boyer. This is my son, Mark," he said, reaching out to shake the man's hand.

"I'm Jim Dillon, pastor of the Tabernacle."

Not Beth's fiancé, Jack Alton, after all. But didn't pastors wear robes? Adam wondered as he shook hands with Pastor Dillon. Dressed in a camel-colored jacket, neatly creased gray wool gabardine trousers and a matching gray turtleneck, the pastor looked as unconventional as his church.

"I was so relieved when Jack said you'd gotten stateside in time to come today," Pastor Dillon said.

"Wild horses couldn't have kept me away."

Pastor Dillon grinned. "But the Navy could have. I'm glad you got free of obligations in time. Elizabeth should have *some* family here. The Taggerts have all but adopted her, but that just isn't the same as real family."

"Our parents aren't coming?" Adam asked, wondering why he was so surprised. Jack had said they didn't approve of the marriage. That was why Adam was there to give her away, but he thought they'd at least attend.

Pastor Dillon shook his head and pursed his lips as if holding back his opinion. "I tried to talk with them, but it was no use."

Adam had run into that particular brick wall enough by the time he left at eighteen to know how uncomfortable the pastor's visit with his parents must have been. "Sorry," he said, still automatically apologizing for them even after years of absence.

Pastor Dillon shook his head and smiled. "It isn't necessary to apologize. Seeing Elizabeth smiling with you at her side is going to be its own reward. And…"

He stopped and cocked his head. "That clip-clop of hooves and jangle of harness tells me she's here."

"Hooves? Harness?"

"She's in a carriage," Mark exclaimed looking out the glass door. "It's being pulled by a horse!"

It was the first glimmer of enthusiasm he'd seen in his son since Adam arrived to retrieve Mark from his aunt Skyler's a week ago. He chuckled at Mark's childish excitement, but then cast a horrified glance at the pastor, realizing Mark's exuberance might be misplaced in a church setting.

Pastor Jim Dillon laughed softly and sent him a commiserating look. "Don't sweat it. My son's almost Mark's age. Besides, we're pretty informal around here. There should always be joy and laughter in God's house."

He looked out toward the carriage and grew serious. "You may remember Ross Taggert. He owns the property next to Boyerton. He's driving the carriage, and that's Cole, his son, with Elizabeth. He's her best friend, and she thinks he's giving her away. Instead he's one of Jack's groomsmen."

"I do remember the Taggerts. Ross used to let me ride his horse. It was the only time I got to ride for pleasure."

Adam gazed out the window at the carriage as it pulled to a stop. He realized his hands were sweating. It had been nearly twenty years since he'd said goodbye to Beth. He didn't think he could handle this reunion with an audience—even if the audience was the most important person in his life. "Mark, suppose

you go grab a seat while I go out to meet your aunt.''
His son looked ready to protest when Pastor Jim Dillon put his hand on Mark's shoulder.

"Come on, Mark. We should give them a few minutes alone after all these years. I'll show you where your father's supposed to sit during the service. You can wait for him there.'' Miraculously, Mark nodded and went without protest.

Adam took a deep breath and opened the door. After a second deep, icy-cold inhale, he started down the walkway toward his blond sister, whom Cole Taggert was helping climb down from the high carriage seat. It was hard to believe his parents would have let her befriend a Taggert. Not that there was a thing wrong with the Taggert family, in his own estimation. But to his father, their poor taste in working hard off the land and not having inherited money was unforgivable.

Apparently Beth hadn't been listening to them for a while. He should have tried to get in touch with her after the first couple of years' worth of letters went unanswered, but he'd assumed his parents had turned her against him. She had been so angry when he left that it hadn't been hard to imagine.

Adam was nearly to the carriage when Cole Taggert noticed him. The younger man winked and, putting his index finger over his lips, sneaked away while Beth's back was still turned.

Beth was having quite a time trying to arrange her heavy silk dress and fur-trimmed cloak while holding her train off the ground. "Cole, you aren't just here to keep me upright on the way down the aisle. Would you give me some help? If I drop this train and get it dirty before Jack sees me, I'll just die.''

She passed him the loop on the train without looking up. Adam took hold of it, smiling. He let all the affection he'd kept in his heart for his little sister pour forth in his voice when he said, "If you're as pretty as I remember, he'll barely notice the dress."

Beth whirled and stared up at him. His pounding heart ached when he saw the blank expression in her eyes. She didn't recognize him after so long.

"It's Ad—" he began, but she blinked and an uncertain smile tipped her lips upward.

"Adam? Adam!" And then she nearly knocked him flat when she launched herself and twenty pounds of silk and pearls into his arms. "You're here! It's really you!" She stepped back and blinked. "Wait. How did you—?"

"Jack got in touch with me. He says to say, 'Surprise!' I'm here to give my little sister away to one very lucky man. As long as you don't think a Navy dress uniform would wreck your wedding pictures."

Blinking back tears, she shook her head. "This is… Oh, thank you so much for coming. You'll never know how much this means to me."

Adam hugged her. "No, Beth. You'll never know what an honor it is to be here for you. I've missed you. So much."

"Oh, Adam, I've missed you, too. You're the only family I have left."

"Then it's their loss. And I'm not the only one

here. I have Mark with me. What do you say we get inside, get you hitched, and then you can meet him?''

''I'd say you still come up with the best plans!''

Adam took her arm and hid a grimace. He hoped this plan for a fresh start for him and Mark was a good one, because his son was furious that the move had yanked him away from his mother's family. So far Adam was the only one who saw its merits. His in-laws were upset that Mark would be so far away and Mark's aunt Sky was hurt and disappointed that he hadn't signed guardianship over to her. Everyone acted as if he'd never wanted to be a father and thought he should have stayed in the Navy. It had been a temptation. The SEALs had been his life, his family for years, but not by choice, and it was time for a change.

For all of them.

Chapter Two

Alexandra slung her coat over her shoulders, hurrying to her car across Indian Creek High School's parking lot. Though she was one of the high school guidance counselors, with Elizabeth away on her honeymoon, Xandra was the contact for New Life Inn. She was on her way to the hospital emergency room to offer shelter and solace to a fearful, hurting woman. She'd gotten the call less than five minutes ago, and luckily she had no meetings scheduled for the rest of the afternoon, so she was free to leave the school.

It hit her then, as she tucked her hair under her hat, how far she'd come from the woman she'd been on that first day of November over a year ago when Elizabeth welcomed her to New Life.

With just a little spring in her step, she continued to her car. Xandra was almost at the edge of the campus where she'd parked when she noticed a puff of smoke drift upward from under the bleachers. She could smell the tobacco from where she stood. Casting a quick look at her watch, she weighed her options. Should she take the time to try putting some class-cutting smoker of an adolescent back on track? Or should she put an adult back on track by rushing off to the hospital emergency room?

Xandra sighed, knowing she couldn't ignore either plea, no matter how unconsciously this immediate one had been made. With a quick prayer for wisdom winging its way to her Lord and Savior, she changed direction and was soon ducking under the bleachers. It wasn't long before she saw him in the shadows— a tall boy leaning nonchalantly against a support pole.

Apprehension speared her. She should have gone to get another teacher. He was so tall. But he's still a child, she told herself sternly and spoke with as much calm as she could muster.

"I'm asking myself why someone would stand in the freezing cold rather than stay in a nice cozy classroom where he just might improve his mind."

"And here I thought I'd avoided this lecture by skippin' health class," the youth grumbled. "Looks like I wasted my time." He crushed the butt under his foot, coughed, then turned to face her.

It was Mark Boyer. He was the nephew Elizabeth had called her about before she left for her honeymoon in Ireland. She'd seen him at the wedding and earlier that morning with his father in the studies office arranging a class schedule. The teen's long, sun-kissed, golden-brown hair stirred in the breeze and framed a face that was going to take the female population of the school by storm, if it hadn't already. He'd gotten his looks from his father, and she couldn't help but wonder if the older version wasn't already making the same impact on the women of the area.

Mark's eyes, she noticed, were the same startling green as Elizabeth's, but what surprised her was the pain and anger she read in them. There was something else too in those oh-so-green eyes and that was gentleness. Oh, it was all gone in the split second it took him to paste on a devil-may-care mask, but it had been there.

Great. Just what she needed. Another troubled teen, and this one from the Boyer family. Xandra and Elizabeth had made their peace and were friends now. Not so the rest of the Lexington and Boyer houses. Adam Boyer had been gone a long time, but when he learned that Xandra's brother, Jason, had raped Elizabeth, his anger would be just as fresh as if it had happened yesterday instead of fifteen years ago. Xandra sighed at the thought of all the anguish and hate her late brother had caused and prayed for an end to it.

"And you shouldn't litter," she collected her thoughts enough to tell young Mr. Boyer.

He shrugged and turned away to walk toward the school.

"Hold on a minute. I don't know how they handle cutting class in New Mexico or California, but here there are consequences, Mark. You may have escaped a health-class lecture this afternoon, but now I own some of your time for the next few days.'' She took out a pad of paper that produced copies in triplicate and filled in the blanks of the form as she spoke. ''Smoking on school grounds earns you a detention. Cutting class the first time means a meeting between me and your father plus the added bonus of a one-day in-school suspension for you. A second skip would earn another meeting for your dad and a whole Saturday working on the grounds, planned for you by our custodial staff. Hopefully you'll have learned your lesson with this first offense. Have your father in my office at nine tomorrow morning.''

She reached forward, took his hand, and slapped two of the three slips in the middle of his square palm. ''Take this to the principal's office, then head back to class. And if you know what's good for you, when I check with the office, I'll find you got there.'' She paused to look at her watch. ''Within, say, three minutes.''

Xandra could see it coming when he opened his mouth to protest. She held up her hand. ''Save the my-father-is-too-busy-for-a-meeting speech. I've heard it at least a thousand times in the last year. Both of you, Mark. Nine a.m. sharp.''

She didn't wait for more protest, but pivoted and walked away. She found herself fighting a smile seconds later as she strode toward her car to the tune of his footsteps pelting toward the building. Three minutes was cutting it pretty tight from that part of the campus. Mark wasn't as rebellious as he'd been trying to look.

Xandra sobered quickly as she slid into her car. The visit with an abused woman named Annie Kline was still ahead, and she prayed even more fervently that she'd find the right words. The woman was in the same sort of trouble she'd been in when she'd struck out a year and a half earlier on the long road that had led to New Life Inn.

Xandra checked her watch again as she hung up the phone. Leaning her head against the wall behind her desk, she closed her eyes and pinched the bridge of her nose, trying to fight off a blossoming headache. She couldn't believe her mother had done this to her. Just one more day and her scheduled meeting with Adam Boyer about his son, Mark, would have been about the smoking and class-cutting incident, and only that. Now, thanks to Mitzy Lexington's activities, it would probably be a confrontation shadowed by the past.

Her mother's call was the first in the three-and-a-half months since she'd learned that Xandra had decided to remain at New Life Inn and work part time for Elizabeth there. Her mother's outrage had been nearly as overblown as her last bout of hysteria. That one had come when she'd learned that Xandra's divorce was final.

For Xandra the divorce had been like a miracle. Her first stop after fleeing her home had been San Diego, California, at a city-run abuse center. There she'd met Virginia Talmadge, a tough old broad of an attorney. Talmadge had devised an ingenious strategy to force Michael Balfour into agreeing to a quick no-fault divorce.

First, the savvy female attorney had filed for a restraining order and had gotten it with the use of pictures of Xandra's bruised and battered face. All it had taken from there was the threat that Xandra would go public with the pictures, ruining Michael's social standing unless he cooperated. He'd agreed to a quick divorce on grounds of his infidelity—which Xandra couldn't prove—instead of being sued on the grounds she could prove.

After the papers were filed, Xandra began to suspect she was being followed. So she'd taken off, heading for home where she'd thought she would be safe with her parents. Once there, of course, she'd confirmed they believed she was the one in the wrong. She'd also learned that Michael's detectives were looking for her.

Knowing Michael had hired detectives had frightened her, but she'd consoled herself that she'd made it to Pennsylvania with complete freedom only six months away.

Even now, though the divorce had been final for several months, her parents' outrage was a huge barrier between them. Still, getting the chance to rant and rave about two more Boyers "invading" town had been enough to break down her mother's most recent wall of silence.

Mitzy Lexington had run into Adam and Mark Boyer at a local restaurant the night before. And in true Mitzy style she'd dealt them the same kind of vitriolic treatment she'd been handing Elizabeth for years. She'd told Adam in plain terms what she thought of his beloved sister—of Elizabeth's supposed "false cries of rape," which hadn't been false at all. Her mother just refused to believe it.

Xandra didn't need to be a witness to know just how it had gone down. The words describing Elizabeth as some sort of modern-day Jezebel would have been loud enough for others to overhear, with any mention of the rape said in a quiet undertone to protect Jason's sainted reputation.

With Elizabeth on her honeymoon, Adam wouldn't find out that his sister and his son's guidance counselor were actually friends now and she doubted he'd believe her. The friendship had been formed and forged for reasons Xandra just wasn't yet able to go into with a stranger, especially the parent of a student. It was her private pain and Elizabeth's. So it looked as if her mother and circumstances had conspired against her again, and Xandra had little doubt that the meeting would be strained at best and pretty ugly at worst.

Neither of which would serve Mark Boyer's interests. Her only chance to salvage the whole mess was to try having Mark assigned to the other guidance counselor. So, with no time to spare, Xandra rushed to Principal Harper's office. The bespectacled, balding principal looked up, then stood as she skidded to a halt in his doorway.

"What can I do for you, Alexandra?"

She handed him Mark's file. "I wondered if you

could assign Mark Boyer to A. J. Charles instead
of me.''

Principal Harper set the file in the middle of his
desk and gestured to the chair across from him. After
she sat, he settled his thin form back into his desk
chair. ''I don't understand,'' he said, a frown carving
a deep furrow between his heavy eyebrows. ''Are you
afraid of the boy? Did he threaten you?''

''No,'' Xandra said truthfully, surprised at the deep
concern in the principal's voice. She'd had a moment
of fear there under the bleachers, but the feeling had
faded. He was a troubled child, no matter how tall
and broad he was.

''If the boy doesn't make you leery, then I don't
understand your request,'' her boss said.

''It's just that I think it might be better for A.J. to
handle Mark, since he has no ties to Mark's family.''

''I'd think your friendship with Mark's aunt Elizabeth would cut through any resentment his father
might feel toward an outsider advising him. In my
experience, any foot in the door is better than none
at all.''

''But—''

He held up his hand. ''If it's your job security
you're worried about, don't. Elizabeth may have recommended you for this job, and her father may have
been my son's riding coach, but I wouldn't have hired
you if I didn't think you could do the job. You've
more than proved yourself this past year. You're the
person who'll get this boy back on track. Go ahead
and make Mark's father as angry as you have to. I

don't care. Now, have you looked at the boy's records?'' he asked.

She nodded.

''Then you know this is one bright kid.''

Xandra had to agree, which created a puzzle of sorts. ''His scores are through the roof. And there's not one hint of any trouble before this, but something's wrong. I can see it in his eyes.''

Xandra knew when Principal Harper looked up from the records on his desk that she'd sunk her own ship with that little hint of insight. Unless she wanted to tell him her reason for believing Adam Boyer would especially resent her—a story that wasn't hers to tell—she'd have to make the best of the situation. She stood with a deep sigh.

''I'll do my best to reach him.''

The principal smiled and got to his feet. ''I know you will. Let me know what you think of the father. If we aren't going to get parental support, I want to be informed.''

Xandra nodded and left, defeated, deflated.

As her office came into view, she saw Mark and his father sitting on the bench outside her door. Adam was dressed in a military uniform and looked formidable in his anger. Xandra sent a prayer heavenward for help as she cleared her throat and tried to swallow her trepidation.

''Good morning, Mark.'' She walked toward Adam Boyer. ''I'm Alexandra Lexington, Mr. Boyer.'' She stuck out her hand, hoping it wouldn't get bitten off.

And the Good Lord and anyone seeing Adam Boyer's expression would agree she had reason to worry.

Adam Boyer stiffened and stood. "That's Lieutenant Commander, Ms. Lexington," he said, shaking her hand but in a very stiff, perfunctory way.

She stepped back, shaken by nerves that suddenly tightened every muscle in her body. There was something about him. Not just his height, or the breadth of his shoulders, or the expected anger in his gaze. It was as if he was a larger-than-life figure who diminished her strength by the very power of his presence. She didn't see how she could handle this situation with any degree of finesse.

Xandra looked away, toward his less-threatening son, and sought to take command of the encounter. "Mark, you can go on to the day detention room now," she told the boy.

He glanced at his father as if for permission.

"Hold up there, Mark. My son tells me the punishment for a second offense of this sort is cleaning the grounds on Saturday. Frankly, I don't see the sense in him sitting in some room doing assignments and not attending class. I'd rather have Mark forgo the suspension and give up a Saturday. Since he was outside polluting his body with smoke, I figure cleaning up a little pollution of the human kind on school grounds will do him some good."

Oh, there was no way he was getting her to agree to that! She was sure Mark could find enough ways to test all their patience without the influence of the Saturday bunch.

Xandra dug deep and found a little extra courage. "Rules are rules, Lieutenant Commander. Mark is expected in Mr. Harper's office ASAP."

It was Adam's chance to look surprised. He blinked as if not used to having his ideas questioned. "Surely you can see my point."

Right on top of your head, she longed to say. Instead she nodded. "Nonetheless, rules are rules." She focused all her attention on Mark again. "Now that you've produced your father, you may report to Mr. Harper. He oversees daytime detentions. Please learn your lesson on this one, Mark. I'm sure you don't want us all to get off to a bad start. I'll see you toward the end of the day for a chat. Mr. Harper's secretary will tell you when to come up to see me."

Mark picked up his books and left without a word to his father. When she looked back toward Lieutenant Commander Boyer, he was scowling at her.

"If you won't cooperate," he all but growled, "I'll go with my son and talk to Harper myself. I imagine he has the power to override your obviously prejudiced decision."

"Please, don't do that." She reached out and grasped his forearm as he started to turn away. He glared down at her hand where it rested on his rock-hard arm. Leashed power once again radiated from him, as if she'd grabbed a live wire. Feeling burned, Xandra snatched her hand back. She caught herself before she retreated more than a step, and forced herself to stiffen her spine, though she did still keep her hands clasped behind her back. It wouldn't do for him to see them shaking.

"I'd like to explain my reasoning now that Mark has gone, and I expect you to take back that remark about my having prejudged him. Believe it or not, I want what's best for him."

"I find that hard to believe after the way your mother spoke in front of him last night. It wasn't what I'd call a warm welcome."

"Do you want people to hold you responsible for your parents' actions? Are you comfortable having your actions judged on *their* deeds and reputations?"

He frowned thoughtfully. "Of course not."

"Then kindly do me the same service. If you'll step into my office, I'll explain why I'm so immovable on the subject of how to handle Mark's punishment." She didn't wait for an answer but walked by him and into her office. Perspiration making her hands slick, Xandra quickly put her desk between them and waited for him to enter before settling in her desk chair. There was no way she was giving him the opportunity to stand there towering over her.

But still, the room seemed to shrink from closet to coffin-size the moment he stepped in. It didn't get better even when he sat down. Xandra swallowed at the sight of the banked anger still in his gaze. She stood, paralyzed for a long moment, her white-tipped fingers bracing her weight against the surface of the desk. A cold sweat popped to the surface of her skin.

He might have agreed to continue the meeting, but he was obviously still incensed over the nasty things

Xandra's mother had said about his sister. Frankly, she couldn't blame him, but that didn't make facing him any easier. Nor did it make it easier that once again one or both of her parents had chosen her late brother's interests over hers.

Some things never changed.

Chapter Three

Adam watched Alexandra Lexington gather her dignity about her like a cloak as she sank into her chair. As a SEAL, he'd been trained to read body language, and hers said he'd rattled her, that she was unsure of herself. Still, she *had* managed, so far, to hold her own. Since an angry look from him had been known to send members of his team scurrying for cover, he gave her high points for courage.

He'd noticed her as soon as she'd approached him and Mark. A very pretty woman, she stood about five-six with an almost too-slim figure. Her shining black hair was tortured into a bun at the nape of her slender neck, and she wore a gray power suit that wasn't quite doing its job.

Her blue-gray eyes had gone just a little dark as he stepped in front of her desk to take the seat she'd indicated, further giving away the effect he had on her. Her slim shoulders had contracted, and she'd dropped her chin just a bit as she sat. He chalked a lot of it up to a guilty conscience.

But not all.

For some reason, they struck sparks off each other, and he didn't understand that at all. A spoiled social- ite who played at a career and messed with the minds and lives of children was hardly his type. Adam told himself he didn't care if or why she was uncomfort- able. It was good that he'd thrown her off her stride. From what he'd gleaned from his run-in with her mother, the Lexington family had put his sister through the wringer over the years.

"First of all, we need to get something straight, Lieutenant Commander," she began, calling him back to the present with a jolt.

Her voice, he noted, was still unsteady, and he hated that it bothered him. He wasn't a man who en- joyed intimidating women. Unless, he reminded him- self, they were the enemy.

"By all means, Ms. Lexington, straighten away." He smiled, but it was not meant as a friendly gesture.

And if the way she blinked and swallowed was any indication, she didn't take it as one.

"I—I didn't go looking for Mark yesterday. I was leaving the school when I noticed smoke wafting up from under the bleachers. It was at a time of day when everyone still belonged in class, so I went to inves- tigate. I would have been derelict in my duty if I had handled what I found any differently—no matter who your sister is."

He'd tried to ignore the pang that little stutter of

hers zinged through him, but it was difficult. He couldn't let her get to him. "I don't have a problem with you writing Mark up," he told her, unconsciously softening his tone. "This time he was wrong. But I won't stand for you carrying on your family's vendetta with Mark as the pawn. The kid is going to have enough trouble adjusting to a whole new life, without that. I also have a problem with him missing even more class time. He's being rewarded for what he did with this suspension because he's avoiding class that much longer. Saturday detention would have been better. Mark hates yard work."

She huffed out a breath. "But he might not hate the other students assigned to it with him. Mark is acting out for what looks like the first time in his life, according to his records. Also, according to his records, you're new at being the custodial parent. I'd say you and this move are probably what he's acting out against. Believe me, you don't want your son hanging out with that group of misfits as a way to get back at you. It could just make a bad situation worse. I don't think you want the police calling you one fine day instead of the discipline office, either. Every one of the Saturday kids is a hairbreadth from exactly that."

Adam felt like a balloon that had met its fate at the point of a pin. He couldn't argue with the truth. Mark was angry at him, at the move, and at the unfairness of the world at large, for that matter. And she knew the students in question.

Still, Mark didn't live in a box. "What makes you think he won't find those kids on his own?"

"He might. But the way the school day is structured, it'll be hard. Our students are grouped according to grade-point average and IQ. There are four tracks, and they circulate in different parts of the building. We also schedule classes using a college-type block scheduling, four majors a semester. An hour and a half a class, three minutes between. That cuts down on between-class chitchat even more."

"Then he won't likely run into the kids who are your regulars in Saturday detention," he surmised.

She nodded.

"So I guess Mark's in one of the upper tracks."

Ms. Lexington blinked. "You don't know that he's one of the more advanced students in the school?"

"Mark lived with his mother and her second husband since he was five. When we've gotten together, it's been for vacations and a weekend here and there. I knew he got good grades, but we talked about other things. Sports. Camping. This past couple of years it's been nearly impossible to see each other. I've been out of the country most of the time." And past that, how did he explain the way Mallory had kept him out of Mark's life as much as possible? He shrugged. "When his mother and stepfather were killed, I was deployed, so I couldn't take him right away. I didn't even get word for six weeks. He stayed with his aunt until I picked him up to bring him here to Pennsylvania with me."

"And Mark isn't happy about the move?"

Did she think he needed it rubbed in? Salt thrown

in the wound? "I'm his father. He'll live where I tell him to live."

Her voice strengthened. "And with that attitude, you'll lose him in two years, if not sooner. I have a few books on communication with teens that might—"

If I haven't already lost him.

Adam stood, refusing to take any criticism from a woman raised by the same people who raised Jason Lexington. "I'll handle my son's adjustment to his new life, thank you. Just you make sure you don't become part of his problems. In fact, I should probably stop by the principal's office and ask for a different guidance counselor for Mark."

She stood now, too. Fire gleamed in her blue-gray eyes. They were pretty eyes, now that he thought about it, but that was of no consequence. To him or Mark.

"I was no more happy about being assigned to Mark than you are. I already tried to have Principal Harper remove me, but you're more than welcome to give it a shot."

"And I'll bet you enjoyed spreading your lies to him."

The fire in her eyes blazed higher. "Principal Harper insists I'm the best person to help Mark adjust here. I failed to change his mind because, short of exposing Elizabeth's private business, I couldn't give a reason. And I refuse to do that to her."

Adam stared at her. She didn't sound like one of Beth's detractors, though it could be an act. She wouldn't want her boss to think she had a personal agenda where a student or his family was concerned.

But if the principal thought she was that good...

The real question was, could she be fair? Could he trust her not to use his son?

His instincts about people were usually pretty good, and she did seem genuinely concerned about Mark. Maybe he should give it a try. He sure wasn't having much luck understanding Mark's erratic mood swings this last week. Of course, around her today, his own hadn't been much better.

"I'll leave things as they are right now, but I'd better not learn you've tried to hurt my son. Good day, Ms. Lexington."

Xandra sank into her chair as Adam Boyer pivoted on his heels and disappeared through her doorway. Her hands were shaking, and she flattened them on the desk blotter to make them stop. How could she have let his anger get to her that way? How could she have let him dominate the conversation? He'd put her on the defensive and kept her there from the moment they met. She hadn't even told him why she was no threat to Mark. She'd failed Mark because she'd let Adam's mistrust keep them from progressing to a point where together they might be able to figure out what had Mark acting out.

Blinking back sad, angry tears, Xandra closed her eyes. *Dear Lord, help me in my meeting with Mark. Don't let me lose sight of Your support and please guide me. Calm me. Guide not just my dealings with*

*this one boy but with all those in need of a guiding
hand. Help me with this anger I feel toward my parents, especially my mother. And, Lord, help with the
angry reaction I have to Mark's father.*

The day sped by after that, as one student after
another dropped by her little office asking advice on
everything from the best colleges to divorcing parents. She hoped she'd handled the latter hot potato in
the right way, but one never knew.

At two-thirty, Mark Boyer sauntered in. She studied him for a moment as the girl she'd been talking
with left, nearly tripping over her own feet because
her gaze was locked on Mark's handsome face. Xandra smiled for what felt like the first time that day.
The girls at Indian Creek would never be the same.

Mark had the same incredible bone structure as
Lieutenant Commander Boyer, and at six feet was
already nearly as tall. With any luck, Mark would turn
out to be a little more reasonable and less intimidating
than his father. One thing was sure, she didn't envy
Mark a bit having to deal with a father like his.

Which, she pointed out to herself with a silent sigh,
wasn't a fair assessment of the man's character. He'd
had preconceived notions of her because of what he'd
just learned about Xandra's family, and she had reacted to his understandable anger.

His anger actually pointed out a positive character
trait. He cared about his sister. He'd certainly been
protective of Mark. And though he cared deeply for
his son, he wasn't one of those obnoxious parents

who thought their children could do no wrong. Parents like hers in regard to her brother.

Her own tongue-tied idiocy had let their meeting get out of hand. She should have taken charge and set him straight with the plain simple truth that she and Elizabeth had managed to build a friendship in the months Xandra had lived at New Life Inn. The only reason she hadn't met Adam at the wedding was that Xandra had attended only the ceremony, hoping her absence would keep the past from intruding on Elizabeth and Jack's special day.

"So, my aunt and your brother got hot and heavy once, huh?" Mark said as what she took to be his opening volley.

Xandra felt an unbelievable calm come over her, even though she felt her face pink up a bit. She hooked a loose hair behind her ear and stared at him, her expression showing not a bit of her own inner turmoil. She opened his file, pretended to glance at it as if familiarizing herself with him. Then she closed it and looked up, pinning him with a direct, no-nonsense look.

"No, Mark," she said quietly. "That is not what happened at all. They call it assault now on the news because rape is such an ugly word, but rape is what my brother did to your aunt. She was fourteen years old. He was eighteen. He was a violent and cruel excuse for a human being, and he nearly destroyed a sweet, shy girl. Your aunt Beth has suffered years of mistreatment because my mother can't see what a loathsome creature her precious son was."

Mark blinked, obviously thunderstruck by her candor. "Oh."

"Exactly. I'm on Beth's side. And, Mark, I'm on *your* side. I've looked over your records and I just don't get it. You've always been a model student. What on earth were you thinking?"

"That I don't want to be here. That this isn't home. I want to go back with my aunt, at least." He emphasized each word as if he'd said it often and had been ignored.

"And you think if you get in enough trouble your father will give up on you and let you live elsewhere? He seems to genuinely want you with him. That's a good thing, Mark. But your father is in the military. He has no choice where he lives."

"We didn't have to come here. He moved us here after he resigned. There's another couple months till it's official. He's making this great big sacrifice. Giving up his career. Doing the *right* thing when I know he doesn't want to do it at all. I don't need him. I never did."

"I don't think this is the way to change his mind. Did you resent his career?"

Mark glared at her. "No. It was cool telling all my friends about my dad the SEAL and that he was always going on top secret ops. He's a hero."

There was truth in his tone, but there was also an undercurrent of resentment. Xandra nodded, trying to decide where to step next without further treading on his already hurt, confused feelings.

"What is your relationship with your dad like?"

"He was never really my father. *Jerry* was my father. He was my soccer coach. He was there cheering me at track meets and softball games, yelling if I talked back."

"And where was your real father during that period. Did he live nearby?"

"He lived in California at Coronado. That's a base where the SEALs are stationed and train. It was about five or six hundred miles away from us."

"Did you see him often?"

Mark shrugged. "Sometimes. He tried to fly me out once or twice a year. Sometimes he'd come get me and we'd go places. But other times we'd plan something and he'd get deployed at the last minute. He couldn't even call to cancel. Like I said, top secret ops. When I was little, I'd get upset, but later I understood that he wasn't trying to be mean. He just wasn't allowed to call. Base command would call after he was already gone. Mom would get mad, even though he couldn't help it. Then she wouldn't let him see me when he got back. And she was even worse about it lately. And he didn't seem to mind."

"But still, you had to have seen him quite a bit over the years."

"Oh, sure. He took me to Disney a few times, the Grand Canyon once, a lot of camping trips to different state parks. Real wilderness stuff. Sometimes we went to ball games or out to dinner when he could get a weekend without canceling at the last minute. We just haven't been together nearly as much as my friends with divorced parents.

"I always separated them in my head," Mark went on with a telling change of subject. "There was Jerry who I called 'Jerry' but he was my father. And there was Adam who I called Dad but he was more like an uncle."

"Did you have a good time with him? Did you get along?"

"Sure, but like I said, it was really more like he was my uncle. An older guy but fun. He took me on adventures. But then he showed up three months after Mom was killed and dragged me across the country to live here. Now he thinks he has to be my father, and the fun uncle is gone."

"Is living with him here really so bad?"

"It isn't even like there's family here for either of us. And he bagged his career. For what?"

"You?" she ventured. When all Mark did was slump a little lower in the chair, Xandra went on. "Could your dad have left you with your aunt? Was she willing to have you live with her?" Mark nodded. "And you were doing okay in school. Getting good grades. Not getting in trouble. So he had no reason to think you'd be a burden to her, did he? No reason to feel undue guilt if he left you there?"

Mark sullenly shook his head.

"Then I'd guess he *wants* you with him. And he must think being with you is worth giving up the Navy for."

Mark sat up, his eyes suddenly alive, shining. "But he wasn't just in the Navy. He was a *SEAL!* Don't you see? You only get to be a SEAL by being the best. Everybody looks up to them. Women ask *them* out. I bet my dad's had a different girlfriend every time I went to see him at Coronado.

"And did you know he went to Annapolis? His parents tried to stop him, but he got in touch with some senator all by himself and the guy helped get him into Annapolis because Dad was so smart. After that, he tried out for the SEALs and made it through BUD/S. They call the last week of BUD/S 'hell week' because it's so hard. Eighty percent don't make it through."

She fought a smile. Adam Boyer was his son's hero. But he'd never been a father, and now that he was breaking out of his hero mold, Mark didn't know what to make of this new man with clay feet.

"Mark, do you talk to your dad? Not about sports or what you're planning to do for vacations together. I mean about really important things like what you're feeling."

Mark blushed. "Guys don't talk about stuff like that."

"Do me a favor, Mark. Tonight, I want you to tell him how you feel about…let's start with something easy, your first detention yesterday. And the suspension today. Will you do that, then come tell me what happens?"

"Why?"

"Because I think your dad loves you and very much wants to be a father to you. He just may not know exactly how to do that on a twenty-four/seven basis. And I don't think you know how to take him as a twenty-four/seven father, either. Relationships take work. They take talking out feelings, not acting them out the way you did yesterday by cutting class to try to force him to send you back to your aunt. He's a very stubborn man. He didn't get through— what did you call it?—hell week without being stubborn. You have to see you're with him to stay. Rather than chance ruining both your lives, I think you'd better try to make the best of it.''

And for Mark's sake, she'd try to make the best of dealing with a man who was larger than life and twice as scary. She just wished she didn't get the feeling that Adam Boyer was somehow going to cause a huge upheaval in her life. One she wasn't sure she'd ever be ready for.

Chapter Four

"**B**oy, it really stunk," Mark said out of the clear blue.

Adam looked up at his son from the uninspiring dinner they were both trying to choke down. There was a hunger in Mark's green eyes that Adam had a feeling had nothing to do with the poor excuse of a dinner. He just wasn't sure he was ready to deal with anything deeper than his own lack of culinary talent.

"Sorry your ol' dad isn't much of a cook. Too many years of at the mess or eating Meals Ready to Eat." He grinned. "And sometimes bugs, if the MRE's ran out on deployment."

"Oh, gross on the bugs." Mark rolled his eyes. "The MRE's you bring on camping trips are lots better than this. Maybe we should find a commissary and get some. But I wasn't talking about dinner," Mark said, waving his sawdust-like burger in the air. "I mean the detention yesterday and sitting in that room

all day today is what stunk. I never had to sit in—"
He hesitated, his smooth forehead wrinkled in con-
centration. "Well, I guess the 'bad chair' is the best
way to describe the way it felt."

"The bad chair?"

"In kindergarten and first grade, kids who caused
trouble had to sit in a special chair in the back of the
class. The bad chair."

Adam grinned. "Sailors have to wash dishes or
paint."

Mark cracked up and dropped his dry burger to his
plate as he looked around the messy kitchen. "Guess
you didn't get into trouble much, either."

Adam laughed. "SEALs do push-ups and run laps.
We're special." Still grinning, he looked around at
the kitchen disaster the small meal—and the others
for a week—had left behind. "I think we're both in
trouble now. We need help. Someone to cook and
clean up this place."

"Yeah. For a while I figured with a house this big,
we could just move rooms when they got too messy,
but there's only one kitchen." Mark tipped his nose
in the air and attempted a British accent. "Rather
foolish of the previous Boyers not to plan ahead with
a few auxiliary kitchens."

"You have no idea how foolish the previous Boyers were and are, son. Someday I might explain some
recent ancient history. In the meantime, let's ditch this
slop and go grab a decent burger at the deli in town.
Then I'll tackle this mess on a full stomach."

"I'll help."

"No. You'll do your homework."

"I did it while I was in the bad chair," Mark said with a shrug. His eyes, however didn't reflect the carelessness of the gesture.

Adam frowned. That wasn't the way the day had been explained in the note he'd been given. "I thought you were supposed to only do the day work assigned today and save homework for tonight."

His tone tinged with defiance, Mark said, "Yeah, well I got done it all early. After I talked to Ms. Lexington and got the assignments for tonight, I did them, too. I figured if they were stupid enough to think it would take me all day to do a few hours' work, they'd never suspect what I was working on."

"Mark, you can't bend the rules to suit you. Rules are rules for a reason." Adam pushed his plate away from himself. "Breaking rules is what got you in trouble in the first place. If you'd been caught, you'd probably have gotten another detention."

Mark jumped to his feet. "You know, for a while I thought Ms. Lexington was right. That telling you how I felt would make you see who I am, but you won't. You used to be fun. Now you're my commander instead of my dad, the way you used to be. Forget dinner. I'm not hungry anymore. I'll go pretend my room is detention and put in my time there."

Adam sighed and took a bite of his cardboard hamburger as Mark stormed from the room. He glared at the unappealing mess and tossed it on his plate. Where had Mark's outburst come from? And why did the kid take offense at the least little correction? Did

Adam really act like a commander, rather than a father? He hadn't been around Jerry and Mark much, but there had been enough contact over the years that Adam had seen Jerry rein Mark in a time or two.

Things had been going so well. Better than usual. He shook his head, remembering something Mark had said. *For a while I thought Ms. Lexington was right. That telling you how I felt would make you see who I am, but you don't.*

So Alexandra Lexington was behind Mark's momentary turnaround. He wished she'd given him the heads-up. Maybe then he wouldn't have blown it with Mark. Again. Maybe then he could have figured out what Mark had been trying to say.

Adam withstood two days of one-word answers from Mark before he called the school and asked for an appointment with Alexandra Lexington on Monday morning. He'd dressed in a pair of chinos and an oxford cloth shirt this time, since he didn't want to humiliate himself along with his uniform.

Swallowing his pride wasn't easy, but he couldn't forget her warnings about the eventuality of Mark being picked up by the police and that his eighteenth birthday loomed only a couple of years ahead. She'd hit a nerve with that one. He himself had walked away from his home and family at eighteen thinking he was a whole lot older than he was. He didn't want to repeat his parents' mistakes or continue on the same path that had led to his own lonely history.

As he walked toward the guidance counselor's office, Adam tried to prepare himself to eat crow. It was contrary to every bit of training he'd been given and everything he'd ever learned, but for Mark he'd do anything. Maybe Alexandra Lexington could help.

Maybe.

She was alone in her little airless cubicle of an office, staring at a small photo book, but her gaze was unfocused. She looked wistful and sad. It was more of the vulnerability he'd glimpsed in their first meeting. It was a vulnerability not reflected by her tweed jacket, white no-nonsense blouse or the classic string of pearls about her neck. But still, there was something more approachable, and a little sad about her today. Feeling a bit like an intruder he cleared his throat.

She looked up. Her glittering eyes met his, and for one moment suspended in time, the rest of the world disappeared—right along with his intellect and powers of speech. He wanted to help erase that sadness and those unshed tears from her blue-gray eyes. But for the life of him, Adam couldn't say one word.

Then she focused on him. Eyes wide, startled and full of a fear he could see, but one she quickly tried to hide from him. Carefully, as if it were a ten-pound hunk of plastique with a hair-trigger detonator attached, she set the little book down and closed it cautiously.

Adam almost asked if something was wrong, if he could help. But he didn't. He had his own problems and he thought his explosive relationship with his son was probably enough of a problem for them to negotiate right then. Apparently she agreed.

"Come in," she said, her expression controlled now. "I was glad to hear you'd called. I saw Mark yesterday. Do you want to tell me what happened, or do you want to hear what he thinks happened?" she went on.

He shrugged, a casual gesture he hoped hid his insecurities at least a little. "I guess I blew it. I don't have a clue how, but I did," he admitted. Pride swallowed, he took a seat.

"Mark says he tried to tell you he felt stupid and embarrassed for what he did, but that you picked an argument with him about something unrelated."

Instantly on the defensive, he said, "I don't remember him saying anything about stupidity or embarrassment, and it wasn't an unrelated topic. I'm probably going to cause more trouble for him by telling you this, but he did his homework during his in-school suspension."

She frowned and went through the file on her desk. "I told you, I'm not here to make Mark's transition difficult. Nothing you say goes past that door or is held against Mark." She gathered a sheaf a papers into her hands. "Frankly, I only care that the assignments were done. You say he had time during the day to do those homework assignments as well as all this? That's incredible. Normally this work should have taken long enough to keep him busy into evening, and then he should have had his homework to tackle. Mr.

Harper was surprised he'd finished all this by the end of the day. And now you're telling me he did more?''

Adam's stomach sank. Now he understood his mistake. "So rather than pick up on the fact that he'd finished all his assignments early, I corrected him for doing his homework, too."

Alexandra Lexington leaned back in her chair. "Well, you did miss a good chance to praise him. But I'm afraid you missed more than that. Mark approached you with his feelings that night. The bad chair? That was his way of saying he felt foolish about what he'd done. That was an opening and—''

"And I missed it." Adam raked a hand through his hair. "Maybe that's why he didn't take the correction the way he would have from Jerry. Jerry Beecham was his stepfather.''

But she was shaking her head again. "I've heard all about his stepfather from Mark. Maybe it would help if you knew Mark saw him as a father figure. He'd separated your roles in his life, you see. You were his fun-uncle figure. Dinners and ball games, trips to Disney, wilderness camping. Day-to-day discipline fell to your ex-wife and her husband, so that's who Mark came to expect it from. From what I gather, he was able to accept it from them. The problem is that Mark is having trouble dealing with you as a father because he barely remembers you as one. You've been something else to him.''

Resentment toward Mallory and Jerry rose to the surface. Once again, as he'd learned after she'd betrayed him, Adam understood how fine a line it was between love and hate. And he really didn't need some stranger telling him about what he'd been denied all these years. "Well, now I'm more," he snapped. "Besides, I've corrected Mark over the years without a problem. Until now, that is."

"Those were probably in circumstances outside everyday life, and as an instructor, in the case of your camping trips."

His spirits at a low ebb, Adam said what he was thinking. "I don't need you to tell me that I haven't been able to be a father since Mallory left."

She blinked at his tone and her back stiffened, but she continued on. "I don't think it's as black and white as you seem to think, and it isn't only about you. Mark has had to fit you in somewhere in his mind and heart all these years. You became his hero, which isn't necessarily a good thing right now."

Now that sounded just plain wrong! "You think it's bad that my son looks up to me? From where I'm sitting, that's the only good news I've had. I came here hoping you could help, but I just don't see where you're coming from. How can that be bad?"

"It's possible that with you two living together, he now sees that you have faults, and he's angry about it. You've toppled off your pedestal. Worse, he seems to think it's partly his fault. I sense he regrets your decision to resign your commission. I think he blames himself, since you did it to be a full-time father to him."

Adam shook his head. "You don't understand. He's angry, but not about my faults. Mark was living with his mother's sister after the accident that killed his mother and Jerry. He stayed there till I could get stateside. Mark wanted to stay with her indefinitely. That's Mark's problem. He didn't get his way. I never gave up my right to be his father—and I won't. But it's not what he wants. And *that's* why he's angry."

"Lieutenant Commander, I'm speculating here. And you must be, too. Mark is so conflicted right now, I'm not sure *Mark* knows why he's angry or what he wants."

"So what's so wrong with me telling him where we're going to live? I refuse to feel guilty for that any longer. It's my job as a parent to see that Mark has the right environment, and it's my right as a parent to take my son where I've decided to live."

She huffed out an impatient breath. "I never said otherwise. Parents move their children all over for flimsier reasons than wanting to return to their hometown. I was only trying to give you some perspective on Mark's feelings. And to explain that you need to listen for little openings and to take advantage of them if you want to have a good relationship with him. Grab on and use any opportunity to explore his feelings and yours. Try to guide, rather than order the way you did with your men, and notice the moments when he's begging for praise, even though he doesn't seem to be. I'm not saying it's easy. But the more important accomplishments in life rarely are."

"A warning would have been helpful," Adam said tersely. "If I'd known he was trying to express feelings, I might have seen what he was getting at. I was choking down dinner and all of a sudden I was in the middle of a minefield with him. I want a warning in the future if you challenge Mark to talk to me about something. As for all this other stuff you said, I'll have to think about it.''

"Fine, but I'd like this talk between us kept confidential for now," she said.

He sat back, crossing his ankle over his knee. "If you're so sure of all this, why don't you want him to know I was here? I'd think knowing I'm concerned for him would help our relationship."

"If you remember, I said I'm speculating—using those clues I mentioned that Mark is casting out. I'm certainly not trying to throw up roadblocks to your relationship. I just don't want him thinking we've been talking about him behind his back."

"Even though we are and he's doing the same thing to me?" Adam asked, annoyed again rather than curious.

She sighed in a way that said she thought he was an idiot. About emotional stuff, he admitted to himself, he probably was.

"Mark might not confide in me if he thinks we're in cahoots, Lieutenant Commander. Don't you want him to have someone to talk to?"

This whole thing was just a little much. Was he supposed to be grateful to this woman for butting into his relationship with Mark? He was willing to take advice, but not to have her as a third party in the conflict between himself and Mark. "He's my son. I want him to talk to *me*.''

She smiled, but it was more of a sarcastic smirk. "But he tried that. Didn't he?"

"Look, you weren't there. Talking about abstract kindergartners having to sit in a bad chair was a pretty darn obscure way for Mark to tell me he felt foolish for his show of rebellion. While you're casting blame, ask yourself why the kid can't express his feelings better than this. And remember, I'm the one who wasn't allowed to be a parent all these years. Maybe Mallory and Jerry weren't the paragons of parenthood everyone has made of them."

He didn't wait for her to do more than raise her perfectly arched eyebrows in that way doctors and commanding officers have of saying *Now, where did all that come from?*

"Good day, Ms. Lexington," he said as he stood and left abruptly, refusing to answer the unspoken question her expression asked. Because the truth was, all that about Mallory and Jerry came from a place of deep-seated hurt and disillusionment caused by Mallory's affair with, and subsequent marriage to, Jerry Beecham. And it was a place he wasn't sure he'd ever be ready to explore.

Chapter Five

Xandra stood in the exercise ring at Laurel Glen Horse Farm, where her friend Elizabeth lived with her new husband, Jack Alton. Seated atop her gray Irish draught horse, Elizabeth's blond hair shone in the sunshine. She looked radiantly happy after a two-week honeymoon and her first week back at home of what must be marital bliss. She was happier and more relaxed than Xandra had ever seen her.

"Elizabeth, are you sure your mother-in-law won't mind me riding her horse?" Xandra asked, hesitant to mount the magnificent reddish-brown quarter horse that Jack had trained and given to his mother, Meg Taggert.

"Meg's the most generous woman I've ever met. She'd lend him to you even if she were here to ride him, which she isn't. You're doing her and everyone here a favor. Fly Boy needs to be exercised while Meg's on her cruise. And what is it going to take to get you to call me Beth? I thought we'd become friends.''

"We have, *Beth*. I just forget, that's all. You've been 'that Elizabeth Boyer' for most of my life,'' Xandra said, smiling to take the sting out of the unfortunate truth.

Beth smiled back. "And now I'm Beth Alton, Jack Alton's wife. I think the Elizabeth part of me died when I became a new person in Christ.''

Xandra nodded, knowing just how Beth felt. Almost lighter than air most of the time. She took a deep cleansing breath. "I love the way that sounds,'' she told Beth. "'A new person in Christ.' Thanks to you, so am I.''

"No. Thanks to God's grace and His Son's sacrifice. All I did was allow myself to be His messenger, the way Jack and Meg were for me.''

"I know all that, but I could just as easily have shot the messenger—so to speak.''

"The way I hear my brother did with you?''

Xandra pulled a face and mounted. She squirmed a bit, partly because she wasn't used to the western tack on Fly Boy and partly because she knew she'd blown it with Adam Boyer.

"So, have you seen much of your brother since he and Mark arrived?''

"Besides at the wedding, you mean? Sure. The day we got back from Ireland, Amelia and Ross Taggert threw us a little family welcome-home dinner. Adam and Mark came. And we saw them again last night,''

Beth said over her shoulder as she turned toward the gate one of the handlers held open for them.

Xandra moved up along next to her and through the gate. She couldn't help wondering how father and son were getting along. "What do you think of the dynamics between them?"

"I'm afraid Adam has his hands full with Mark. It's hard to watch. And sad. My brother isn't happy and my nephew is miserable. It was obvious that first night we got back, so we decided to take dinner over last night, hoping maybe we could help. Knowing Adam rode as a boy, Jack invited them over for a ride, thinking they might find common ground." Beth grimaced.

"They aren't coming?"

Beth bent down and opened a gate to a long wide pasture. After they'd both passed through, she locked it again and brought Glory up next to Xandra. Her friend looked a bit troubled.

"Adam wasn't very enthusiastic over the idea, but Mark certainly was." She frowned, looking thoughtful. "But I'm afraid it was only that Mark saw Adam's attitude toward riding and adopted the opposite one."

"Why would your brother be so contrary? I seem to remember he took several junior championships."

"Adam competed until he was about Mark's age. But Father turned riding into constant practice and perpetual competition for him. It was like a job for Adam, not the joy it should have been."

"He did the same thing to you, right?"

Beth nodded. "Adam threatened to start losing badly if Father didn't let him quit eventing. Father was trying to build his own reputation as a coach then and he knew Adam meant what he said, so he gave up. But he also took away Adam's horse and sold it. Adam acted as if he didn't care, but I know he was upset over losing Lancelot. Apparently, he rarely got to ride just for enjoyment."

"Where was your mother while all this was happening?"

"Oh, she was there. Until then Adam had been the rope in a subtle tug-of-war between our parents. She was thrilled Adam wasn't riding anymore. She'd always pressured him about school and his grades."

Xandra felt a little thrill that the lieutenant commander once hadn't been so perfect in school himself. She smirked. "School problems?"

"Adam? Never. School was his refuge. That much I remember. My brother always had a book in his hand. Remember, I was only eleven when he left to join the Navy."

Xandra thought of her life at eleven, and growing up with a brother like Jason. The subtle pinches under the table when she said something he didn't like at dinner. The way he'd corner her and threaten to choke her if she screamed. She'd lived in terror of her brother until he was sent away when she was sixteen. Her own selfish exaltation that she was free even though it meant a younger girl had been hurt was not one of her finer moments.

But she was trying to make up for all that now.

Helping Beth's nephew would go a long way toward easing her aching conscience.

"So things got better?"

Glory, Beth's mount, sidestepped, bumping into Fly Boy. It took a moment to settle both horses. Xandra anxiously waited for an answer.

"All I knew at the time was that the battles between Adam and my parents stopped. Their relationships never recovered, though. I think the Navy represented freedom from our parents' single-minded expectations for him. Adam wants so much more for his relationship with Mark than he had with our parents. That's what makes this all so sad."

Xandra grimaced. "I'm sorry life was so hard on him, but I confess I can sort of identify with Mark. Your brother is this larger-than-life figure, and I can't seem to keep a conversation with him on target. I try to get my point across kindly, but it's hard to be kind when…he…he makes me so nervous."

Beth stopped and turned in her saddle. She stared at Xandra for a long probing moment. "Not all men are abusers. Strength can be controlled. And not all control is bad. One other thing I remember about my brother is his innate goodness. Even though he's probably led a very violent life as a SEAL, I know in my heart that he isn't someone you need to fear physically."

Xandra shrugged. She was disturbed by how much she wanted to put stock in Beth's memories of Adam. She herself had known the truth about her enormously popular brother's hidden faults. But Adam had been gone a long time and, as Beth had just admitted, he'd lived what must have been a violent life. That had to have left a mark on him.

"No offense, but your brother's past is of no consequence to me. Mark is my only concern. For his sake I'll be happy if Adam can be trusted, but I shouldn't have that much to do with your brother. My interaction with any parent is minimal."

"Still, you need to learn to trust your judgment again."

"Your brother's very angry and it makes me uncomfortable and unsure. I also left out that he annoys me and I don't even know why. Between nerves and annoyance, every time we meet, I say the opposite of what I want to say. In the two conferences we've had, I didn't just fail to say all I should have. Out of the blue he made me mad, and then, instead of continuing to cower like a ninny, I lost my patience altogether and said things I shouldn't ever say to a student's parent. Which, of course, made him mad. I'm just lucky he didn't complain to Mr. Harper."

Beth nodded and started her mount forward again. Once again Xandra kept pace with her.

"Something else I remember about Adam is that he fights his own battles. I don't think life as a SEAL has changed that too much. He'd never go to your boss and endanger your job unless you hurt Mark, so I don't see that happening."

About ten minutes later when they topped a hill overlooking an imposing home, Beth pulled to a stop and pointed. "That's Boyerton. I was so shocked when Adam told me he was the one who'd bought it. The first question I asked was how on earth he could afford it.''

Xandra stared off into the distance at Boyerton and suppressed a shiver. She had never seen brick and gray stone look so cold and dour. No wonder Mark called it a mausoleum. Her first question would have been, why would Adam buy it? "Everyone wonders,'' she said instead. "I'm sure he was paid well enough as a SEAL, but rumor has it your parents' estate went for more than four million dollars.'' Xandra grinned. "With that kind of money on the table, I just might enlist.''

Beth laughed. "Actually, it was four-point-two million. And Adam paid cash under the guise of a corporation he uses for investments.''

"You mean he hid his identity from your parents? Wouldn't they have given him a better price if they knew it was him? Surely they wouldn't still carry a grudge because he didn't go to the college they wanted him to.''

"Don't kid yourself,'' Beth said. "My father would have refused to sell to him, unless, of course, he thought he could hit Adam up for money and still keep Boyerton.''

"I still think Navy life is looking pretty good—or at least lucrative.''

A look of pride took over Beth's pretty features. "Mark isn't the only Boyer who's positively brilliant. Adam invented some sort of goggles the U.S. troops use for night warfare. One of the things he did with the money the patents brought him was invest in the businesses retiring SEALs wanted to start.''

''I take it those were wise investments.''

Beth grew thoughtful. ''Apparently, but I get the idea he didn't do it for the money. Some of those men retired because they were injured. He wanted to make sure they had a good life and that their new dreams could come true.''

''What a shame he can't give his son the same kind of break.''

Beth whistled. ''He really has put a burr under your saddle.''

''There I go again.'' Xandra groaned and squeezed the bridge of her nose. ''I'm so sorry. I don't know why I said that. I don't even think he's particularly hard on Mark. And I'm sure he wants Mark to succeed at whatever he chooses to do but...''

''You remind me of myself when I first met Jack.'' Beth chuckled. ''I'll tell you all about our stormy beginning sometime. But right now I think you need a good hard ride to get rid of some of that tension. You'll be sorry tomorrow, but tonight you'll sleep like a baby. Race you to the barn!''

Xandra stared after Beth. Beth and Jack? There was absolutely no comparison between a newly wedded couple and Adam Boyer and herself. None at all. The very idea was preposterous!

Fly Boy took off into a full gallop, almost unseating her. It was a quarter horse trait that Jack Alton had warned her about. After a moment's anxiety, though, she found it exhilarating and laughed with sheer joy as they flew across the meadow.

This was living and she didn't need or want a man in her life. She was happy and fulfilled just the way she was. Xandra turned her mind to the simple happiness that life was now. She had been thinking of buying a horse and boarding it at Laurel Glen. Now she was sure. And she'd found the breed she wanted. She would talk to Jack about it when they returned to the compound. She grinned. Her parents would be scandalized if she bought a working horse that used western tack and boarded it at Laurel Glen. But she gave a mental shrug. Their opinion was their problem. Their stand on her divorce had freed her of living her life to please them.

Freedom.

That's what Beth had said the Navy had meant to Adam. The need for freedom from oppressive family expectations was something she could easily understand. Perhaps in that common thread they could find a common ground and unite to help his troubled son.

"Why didn't you give me your report card yesterday, son?" Adam asked Mark on Saturday afternoon when he found it lying on the kitchen table.

"Didn't think it mattered much." Mark shrugged. "It looks like all the rest always have."

Adam stared at Mark's report card. How could the kid who was driving him so crazy, who slammed doors, tossed his dinner in the trash and stormed out of the house on an almost daily basis, and refused to wear anything but clothes three sizes too big for him, bring home a perfect, model-student report card after only three weeks in the school system?

And why did his son's accomplishment make him feel like such a failure?

After what he knew was too long a silence, Adam said, "You're doing so well in school." He hoped he'd kept the defeat out of his voice. "I'm proud of you, son. I wish you were still in kindergarten. I'd hang it on the fridge."

A shadow crossed Mark's face. "Did you do that? When you and Mom were still married, still happy? Were you ever around back then?"

"I was there as much as I could be. Actually, for every single report card that year till…"

"You left and then we left. What happened to the house? Was it on base?"

Adam would never forget that last hug he'd gotten as a full-time father. He had left for an exercise a father and had come back as something less. While he'd been gone, his wife had run off with some other guy. He hadn't figured out who he was in Mark's life until Alexandra Lexington told him in that last meeting they'd had.

"Dad?" Mark was frowning at him. "Don't you even remember where we lived?"

"Of course I do. I loved that little house. We bought it because your mother didn't want to live on base. She said she wasn't in the Navy, I was. I sold it and sent her the proceeds. Buying it was her idea. I wanted you to have the benefits." To start your new life with another man as your father. "Why do you ask?" he asked carefully, trying to keep his building anger under wraps.

Mark stood up and looked over at the blank slate of the refrigerator. His expression was even more vacant and far away. Adam was just about to go over and tack up the computerized sheet—the new-millennium version of a report card—that showed Mark as the top-ranked student in his grade, when Mark said, "I missed my room, so Mom found me the same wallpaper when she married Jerry."

Knife to the heart! His son had missed his wallpaper. Not his father. Message received loud and clear. Saint Mallory had saved the day and he'd been…replaceable. By another man. By familiar wallpaper.

Recognizing his anger as hurt, Adam let the pain roll across him. He was well versed in hiding hurt. He'd learned it from the cradle. Standing, he followed his instincts and tacked the sheet onto the refrigerator with the magnet from the local pizza parlor that kept them fed these days. He hoped his instincts were right, since instincts were all he had. That and trying to do the opposite of what he knew his parents would have done in any given situation.

"There," he said, stepping back to admire the sight he'd missed for so many years. "Who cares how old you are? It looks right on the fridge. I promise if you have a friend over, we'll take it down."

"I don't have any friends. Or haven't you noticed?" Mark growled.

"You just haven't come across anyone who shares your interests yet."

"That's what Ms. Lexington says."

Adam gritted his teeth. *Ms. Lexington says*— How many times in the last three weeks had he heard that? She was the reason Mark's report card made him feel so defeated. She had done what Adam couldn't. Mark had settled down in school, had received high praise from all his teachers. At home it was a chorus of *Drop dead, Dad. Stuff it. Whatever. I'm going to my room.*

"So what interested you in New Mexico besides schoolwork? What did you guys do on weekends?"

"Whatever."

Adam decided maybe he needed to be a little less of a whipping boy. Ms. Alexandra Lexington's advice wasn't getting him anywhere. He kept listening for the clues she'd told him to, and every time he found one and responded to it, Mark slipped that stiletto tongue of his right through his heart. It was time he started following his own instincts for a change.

"I don't know what 'whatever' means, Mark. What did you do on a typical weekend?" he pressed.

"I played softball and ran track. I'd just gotten into basketball when they—" Mark stopped and took a breath, looking close to tears. "We all went to my games or meets on Saturdays or helped raise money for the teams."

"Have you thought about trying out for sports here?"

"The teams are full. Sorry," he snapped, "I'm not

into sitting on the bench hoping some other guy breaks an arm or a leg.''

Adam arched his eyebrows and leaned against the counter. ''Can't say I blame you. So what else did you do? Track and softball don't run year round,'' he said, avoiding any mention of basketball since it clearly reminded Mark of the accident.

''We were a family. We did family stuff.'' Mark had been getting testy, but now his tone changed. Wistfully, he said, ''Sometimes we'd just go to the mall and laugh at Mom trying on really bad clothes. She never bought any of them, but there was nothing like seeing conservative Mom prancing around in a leopard miniskirt and leather vest.''

Conservative? Mallory? She must have changed over the years without Adam noticing. Most of the time when he'd stopped to get Mark, she'd had on jeans and a shirt. That was almost an American uniform, so it told little about her wardrobe or style.

''So what else did your…family do?'' This was such a weird conversation, but maybe it was the right route. At least it had lasted three times longer than most of their conversations did. When Mark stayed silent, Adam coaxed, ''You have to tell me. I didn't have a normal American family, Mark. I don't have a clue what one does.''

Mark eyed him like a bug under his microscope or an alien life-form. Adam didn't care. They were still talking.

''We'd go to a movie,'' Mark said at last. ''Or Jerry and I'd do yard work or build something together. He had a primo wood shop. Mom would bring us lunch and sit eating hers while we worked. Sundays we'd go to church. Sometimes have an early dinner there. We had a great life.''

''Maybe we should try church. Would you like that?''

Mark shrugged, looking conflicted. ''I don't know. God took away my great life. Why should I worship Him? Or listen to made-up promises about Him?''

''I don't have a clue. But it'd be something for us to do together. Something families do. Even mine did.''

''I did belong to our church's youth group. We did some cool things together,'' Mark said, looking a bit interested.

''Maybe that's where you could meet some kids. Ms. Lexington made it sound as if your school schedule was so tight you'd hardly ever have time to meet and talk to other students except on the bus. And you don't take the bus.''

''Sorry you have to drive with me every day. If this stupid state didn't have a six-month learner's permit rule, I could just take the car.''

''Hey, I don't mind. Teaching your kid to drive is a rite of passage for parents.'' Except for those long, torturous, silent trips back and forth.

''How was your day, son?''

''Peachy.''

''Learn anything interesting?''

''That the Gestapo sometimes interrogated prison-

ers for days. They lost the war. Take the hint, will you?''

Then silence. Deadly, nerve-racking silence would fill the car. What was he doing wrong?

"So we'll go to church tomorrow, but not the one I went to. I'm not sure they'd be ready for either of our wardrobes even in this day and age. How about your aunt Beth's church? Apparently jeans and tees are more than accepted, they're expected. Then we could go over to Laurel Glen and see what you think of riding." For Mark's sake, he'd even put up with the memories that would evoke.

Mark stood looking agitated, almost…threatened. "We'll see. I have a report I need to get on. Can I go now?"

"Sure. I didn't mean to keep you so long. I have to make a call. I had an idea about someone who might be interested in the cleanup-crew job we talked about."

"You mean a maid or a butler or something."

"I was thinking of a guy I served with. Sully's a fair cook and his place on base looked a whole lot better than this place is starting to look."

"Whatever," Mark said, and walked out.

Adam watched him go, wondering what had just happened and if there was a way to officially strike *whatever* from the English language. He felt buoyed and deflated at the same time. For a while there they had really "communicated," as Ms. Lexington would call it. But now that the conversation had fallen apart, Adam felt once again bereft of the company of his son. And worse. As if there had been something deep going on in Mark's head and he'd once again failed to tune in to it, as Ms. Lexington would also point out.

Maybe if Mark found some friends. Maybe at Beth's church. Maybe he'd be Mark's hero again for thinking of the idea. Yeah, tomorrow they'd go to church. Mark would meet nice kids and Adam would win points. Alexandra Lexington hadn't helped Mark find friends. After tomorrow he'd be ahead.

"Wait a minute," he muttered aloud. "When did this Lexington woman get to be my opponent in a contest for Mark's affections?"

Chapter Six

"Adam, Mark, welcome to the Tabernacle," Pastor Jim Dillon said as he offered his hand to both of them in greeting. The pastor was standing on the sidewalk leading to the front door of the barn-church. He was dressed even more informally today in jeans and an open bomber jacket that showed off a shirt with a decidedly Hawaiian twist. It look as if Adam and Mark weren't underdressed in their jeans and tees. Maybe choosing this church really had been a good idea.

"Do you want to attend services with your father or head on over to the youth hall?" the pastor asked Mark as the two shook hands.

Mark's "Whatever" reply had Adam cringing.

Jim Dillon, however, chuckled and glanced Adam's way with a wink before he said, "Definitely the youth group service. Mark, if you follow that path back around the side of the church you'll see the door to our youth hall. In fact, there's my son. Hey, Ian,'' Dillon shouted to a dark-haired kid walking toward the far end of the barn. ''Come here. There's someone I want you to meet.'' Still grinning, the pastor told Mark, ''He can show you the way and introduce you to the whole motley crew.''

Mark turned and watched Ian Dillon, his gaze wary and hopeful at the same time. As the kid drew closer, Adam could see that Ian looked a lot like his father. Ian was about Mark's age but by the time he reached them, he was huffing and puffing like an old man.

''You okay?'' his father asked, concern written on his features as he laid his hand on Ian's shoulders.

''I had to round up the twins for Mum. They ran off for the woods so I had to give chase,'' the teen said in some sort of diluted British accent. ''This cold air's got me. That's all, Dad. I'll be right as rain once I get inside.'' He turned toward Mark. ''So, hi. I'm Ian…but I guess you figured that out by now. And you are?''

''Mark Boyer.''

''Hello, Mark. Come along, then. Meet the rest of us. Prepare yourself for a treat. We're the absolute best Chester County has to offer. Our moderator…''

''Your son seems like a nice kid,'' Adam said after the two moved on and Ian's slightly halting conversation faded.

Jim Dillon smiled as he watched the boys make their way toward the smaller building. ''Ian's a great kid. He isn't supposed to exert himself in the cold but it's hard to keep him down. These frigid temperatures aren't too good for his asthma. So, you decided to give our congregation a try," he continued, looking back to Adam once more.

Adam wanted to put a quick end to Pastor Dillon thinking he'd found a new, dedicated member for his flock. "Mark's mother and I were divorced. Apparently, she and her husband took him to church, so I thought I should, too. They were killed recently, and Mark's with me. He's not meeting other kids since I brought him east. I thought a church might be a place he'd meet some nice kids."

Grinning broadly as if enjoying a private joke, Jim Dillon reached out and clapped him on the shoulder. "I've heard slimmer excuses. I don't care why you came and, believe me, neither does the Lord," he assured Adam. "Hope you enjoy the service."

Adam was still wondering what the pastor had meant when he noticed an approaching couple surrounded by a horde of children. Jim Dillon smiled and raised his hand in greeting.

Considering the distraction a reprieve, Adam beat a hasty retreat and took a seat at the back of the sanctuary. He looked around the structure, once again admiring the imagination it had taken to envision carving a church from an old barn. Then, before he knew it, a band began playing an upbeat tune much like the ones that had been played at Beth's wedding. He shook his head. A barn and a rock band. Who'd have thought of this as a church setting?

Jim Dillon made a few announcements, cracked a couple of pretty amusing jokes, and then asked everyone to open to Matthew 6:26 "Look at the birds of the air, for they neither sow nor reap nor gather into barns, yet your heavenly Father feeds them. Are you not of more value than they?" he began. Interspersed with the dry wit Adam assumed was a trademark, Jim Dillon endeavored to convince his congregation that God cared about them and could certainly be counted on for help because He was as indulgent as any good father.

That, Adam thought as he looked from smiling person to smiling person, was probably fine for these people to believe. God had obviously given them good lives. And judging from the peaceful, happy expressions on the faces he saw, they hadn't seen the side of life he had or had their safe comfortable lives turned inside out and upside down as often as he had. He doubted there was a man there who had ever come home one day to find his wife and child gone without a warning.

Maybe he'd been blind not to have seen how unhappy military life was making Mallory. Maybe he'd been wrong not to take notice of her restlessness when he returned home after missions. Maybe, because he had missed the signs, he'd even deserved the end to his marriage. But he didn't think he had deserved the way she'd done it.

He'd come home on a stretcher, seriously considering retirement lest his son grow up without a father—lest his wife have to raise Mark alone. Then he'd awakened to find not his loving wife but his base commander standing by his hospital bedside with a short note from Mallory. She'd explained in only a few words that life as he'd known it was over. That his son would have another father now. That her lawyer would contact him in regard to the dissolution of their marriage and division of property. That he was alone once again.

Mallory had literally run off with a sailor who'd recently been discharged, and she had replaced Adam with him. Adam still wondered if he would have been able to lure her back with a promise that he'd leave the SEALs for her. Leave the Navy altogether. But pride, hurt and anger had stopped him. She clearly didn't need him. She'd even found a new father for Mark. Rather than retire, Adam had worked toward his physical recovery with single-minded intent and he'd made the SEALs his family, advancing through the ranks to command his own team.

And Mark grew up without you, he berated himself silently. *Now, when your kid needs you, he doesn't even know you and you sure don't know him.*

Of course, part of the problem was that Adam didn't know who he was himself these days.

''Excuse me,'' a soft female voice said, calling him back to the present. Adam blinked, then a disquieting feeling descended as the voice he'd heard penetrated the fog in his brain. He looked up and into the startled eyes of Alexandra Lexington.

Well, there you go. Murphy's Law strikes again. Mark's gonna love the kids in the youth group and I'm gonna run the risk of seeing her every single Sunday.

And be annoyed.

He stood to let her by. He didn't have a choice if he didn't want her standing there staring down at him like a bug under a microscope. In the instant it took for her perfume to fill his senses, the truth smacked him upside the head. His edgy reaction to her had more to do with attraction than irritation.

He stood transfixed by her startled eyes. Right then they looked more ice-blue than blue-gray. Her gaze, he realized with a second flash of insight, was wary but interested in spite of her anxiety. And with that knowledge came a internal kick to his solar plexis the likes of which he hadn't experienced during the toughest combat.

Adam was horrified. He prized loyalty over every other virtue. How could he feel this for a Lexington— one of the people who had clearly persecuted his sister for years? And she was the woman luring his son's affections away from him.

Or was he just jealous that she seemed to like Mark, yet had loathed *him* on sight?

Xandra swallowed hard and dragged her gaze from Adam Boyer's vibrant green eyes. "I really must get by," she told him, scrabbling for composure and losing ground quickly. Why would she notice the verdant color of the man's eyes, especially when seeing him unexpectedly rattled her so badly? And worse, now she realized that her heart had begun pounding and her pulse throbbed and it was all spawned by his intense stare and sudden nearness.

Then he blinked as if coming out of a trance—or at least a fascinating introspection—and stepped into the aisle to let her pass. "Sorry," he said, an embarrassed scowl settling on his face. "I was deep in thought," he continued. "I hadn't realized it was time to leave."

Since he'd sat through a rousing hymn following Pastor Jim's sermon, his thoughts must have been deep indeed. Funny, she'd thought of him as a man of action and certainly not in the least introspective. How else could he continue to misread Mark as he did?

"It's okay," she told him, unaccountably touched by his undisguised chagrin. "Pastor Jim's sermons are supposed to provoke reflection. He stays up front in case anyone wants to talk over their thoughts."

"I think for myself. I don't need the good pastor to judge my motives and insights."

She refused to let him rile her. Or scare her. "When I first came here, I thought faith was a private thing, too. But I've learned that sharing thoughts with people of like mind is more liberating than confining. Believe me, I value my freedom too much these days to give away even a scrap of it. I assume Mark is with the youth group?"

"It's the weekend, you're off duty. Where Mark is isn't any of your concern."

"No. It isn't. Tell me, do you always attack people who are only trying to help you? A simple 'Thank you, Xandra, for helping my son get acclimatized to a new and strange school' would be a little more than in order. You know, you rank up there with some of the most insufferable men I've ever met. No wonder Mark's so miserable. All I can say is that Beth must be blind.''

She didn't give him a split second to respond. Xandra pivoted and left him there with his mouth hanging open. It wasn't until she stomped past Holly Dillon and her two-year-old twins without stopping to cuddle one of them that Xandra realized he'd done it again— sparked a shamefully angry response from her. He'd stolen her peace. Robbed her of her joy.

Why? How?

Remembering her conversation with Beth about her brother, she realized she couldn't put off thinking about why she reacted to him the way she did. Something Beth had said suddenly flooded her mind. *You remind me of myself when I first met Jack.*

Her body went hot, then cold. ''Oh, no. That's not possible,'' she gasped as she got behind the wheel of the New Life Inn's discreet SUV. ''I'm not attracted to him. I'm not!''

But as she steered carefully through the lot, she saw Adam waiting for Mark at his car and felt her pulse once again take off at too fast a rhythm.

''What are You doing to me, Lord? I don't want a man in my life. Never, ever again. Especially a man who is so much a…a *man*. He's too big. Too bold. Too charismatic.''

And maybe, just maybe that's why he scares me.

Chapter Seven

Xandra steered out of the Tabernacle's lot and shifted uncomfortably in her seat. She was a little stiff from riding, but that didn't account for the fact that her nerves were stretched to their limits or that a headache bloomed behind her eyes. No, those particular annoyances could be laid at the feet of Adam Boyer alone.

He disturbed her. Agitated her. Unnerved her. And just plain scared her silly. All for no reason. He was just the parent of a boy she was trying to help and the brother of a dear friend. There was no reason to fear him and none for her to see him except in passing. But his image still swam before her eyes.

What she needed to help her forget her problems was another ride on the amiable Fly Boy. It was a little cold today, but she'd willingly brave more than frigid temperatures to ride off this awful tension that had her in its grip.

Decisively, Xandra pulled over and called Beth on her cell phone. Not a minute later she accelerated back onto the road and headed toward Laurel Glen, excited about the day ahead. She was going to get her first lesson on how to care for her horse—when Jack found her one—and then she was going riding on God's beautiful Sunday.

It took only minutes to get to Laurel Glen but during the drive she could feel her nerves loosen and her headache ease. When she turned off Indian Creek Road and passed under Laurel Glen's landmark iron archway, she realized her headache was completely gone. As she tooled along the lengthy drive to the stables where she was to meet Beth and Jack, however, a worrisome thought struck her.

What if Adam and Mark decided today was a good day to take Jack Alton up on his offer of a riding lesson?

She longed to ask that very question when she met up with Beth and Jack, but she couldn't. She shouldn't be thinking about a student's father on a bright Sunday morning. If she asked she'd risk giving away her inner turmoil and mistrust of Adam Boyer, and Beth would know.

Then Jack opened the stall door and her excitement renewed itself even if Adam and her confusion over him didn't recede completely.

"Since you're serious about horse ownership, I'll feel a lot better with you learning a little care and feeding," he said. "Horses look sturdy and indestructible but the truth is they're pretty delicate creatures.

Beth mentioned that, while you've never cared for one, you did once own a horse.''

Xandra could only nod, remembering with a sharp pang that selling Rain had begun the whole nightmare with Michael, even if she hadn't known then. After all this time the memory still hurt more than she would have thought. When would she be able to let it all go? Put it completely behind her?

''I—I sold him,'' she finally forced herself to say, her voice reflecting some of her anguish. ''We had our own stable when I was growing up, but my parents wouldn't let us help with the horses. Mother said mucking stalls and currying our horses was unseemly.''

But then her emotions took over and a cold sweat suddenly gripped Xandra's body; her thoughts sank into the mire of the past. Michael had objected even more strongly than her mother about her love of riding. It had taken over a year of knowing him for Xandra to learn how much more strongly. He'd thought a woman riding was improper, indecent.

She'd sold her beloved Rain at Michael's insistence, just before they married. His reasons had sounded so logical: Rain's age and the strain of the cross-country trip on the animal. Also, that there was nowhere to ride at the vineyard—a complete lie, she'd learned when she'd arrived at his home after their honeymoon. There she'd found a barn that could have housed Rain and plenty of space for a corral and lots of open area to ride. It wasn't long before she understood that selling Rain had been Michael's first move toward controlling her. His first test.

And in passing his test, she'd failed herself.

Then she'd gone riding two weeks after she arrived in California at a nearby horse ranch, not realizing how strange and twisted Michael's feelings were. When she'd returned, he'd been waiting, furious, uncontrollably angry. It was the first time he'd hit her.

But he'd been so apologetic later. There'd been a problem with production. A day-labor dispute, as well. He hadn't gotten her message at first, so he'd worried terribly. Then he'd worried more when he'd learned she was riding. Horses were dangerous. He'd been in a panic for hours over her safety. She must never ride again. She was too precious for him to lose.

She'd foolishly folded and forgiven him. She'd passed his second test and once again failed herself. She had promised not to ride anymore, just as he'd promised never again to raise a hand to her in anger.

It hadn't been Xandra who'd broken the promise.

"But now you've started over and a horse is your next step forward," she heard Beth say from what sounded like a long distance away.

Xandra found Beth's hand on her shoulder and Jack Alton staring at her as if she were a bomb about to go off.

"Hey! Anyone here?" a voice called from the door of the stable.

Xandra's heart, already beating double time, picked up its pace. *Adam.*

She was just about to beg off for the day, when Jack called out, "In here and just in time."

"Just in time for what?" Mark asked as he walked down the aisle toward them.

"Your riding lesson," Beth said, and shot Jack a look. "He can learn about saddles and the like next time. Let's get him on horseback and make him fall in love with riding first. He needs something he can share with Adam. I'll show Xandra around the barn and give her the first care and feeding lesson, okay?"

"No problem, sweetheart," Jack said, and grinned indulgently over his shoulder at his wife as he stepped out into the aisle. "I have the perfect horse for you to ride," he told Mark. "She belongs to our trainer, C.J. C.J.'s away and the mare needs to be ridden. Her name's Morning."

"A girl horse?" Mark asked disdainfully.

Jack grinned. "You could always ride C.J.'s husband's gelding. Cole wouldn't mind at all."

"No, he will not ride Mischief," Beth said, swatting playfully at Jack's cowboy hat over the stall door.

She stepped into the aisle and swung the wood-and-iron door closed, shutting Xandra inside, giving her time to regain her equilibrium. Through the iron filigree topping the stall walls Xandra saw Beth give Mark an affectionate hug and the boy blush scarlet.

"A lot of men ride mares, Mark," Beth told her nephew. "There's no stigma attached to it. Believe me, you don't want to ride Cole Taggert's horse. He's too temperamental for a beginner...as my husband well knows. Jack's just teasing you, something he does to everyone.''

Mark nodded and turned, following Jack back down the aisle, their boots clomping on the Belgian block floor. He stopped just past Fly Boy's stall, never having seen Xandra. She felt foolish. She should have said hello to the boy. If he saw her now, he'd think she'd been avoiding him, that she was interested in him only because she was paid to advise him during school hours. She reached out to Fly Boy, ran her hands over his neck and down his white blaze. It wouldn't do for the quarter horse to start demanding attention of the newcomers.

''Aren't you taking lessons too, Dad?'' Mark asked in a tone that said he'd decided Adam's reluctance to ride was out of fear.

Apparently, Mark was still looking for a chink in his father's armor. Through the slats of Fly Boy's stall and those of the next one along the row, she could see Adam, and she understood the look that crossed his features. It was only there for a moment, quickly masked with a cocky grin, but Xandra knew what she'd seen. The only thing that scared Adam Boyer was failing at fatherhood. She wondered what would happen if Mark figured that out.

Before Adam could respond to Mark's gibe with more than a pasted-on grin, Jack said, ''Whoa, Mark, I don't think I could teach your father a thing about riding no matter how long it's been since he was on a horse. Get your aunt Beth to show you the scrapbook she has on your father's riding career.''

Adam turned to Beth, a look of such love and yearning on his face that it brought tears to Xandra's eyes.

"You kept some of the stuff I left behind?"

"I'd forgotten all about it. Jack's the one who had to carry it here when I moved from Boyerton." Beth crossed to her brother and they embraced. "Some of it got a little mutilated before I found it," she admitted, her voice muffled by Adam's shoulder until she stepped away. "I rescued it from the trash after Father had your room cleaned out. Maggie was my lookout and I was an eleven-year-old cat burglar. It was a great adventure."

"Maggie was big on providing adventures," he said, and blinked, his eyes going misty.

Xandra felt even worse now intruding on a private family moment. In a way she was glad, though, because seeing Adam so vulnerable over the old woman Beth had supported and cared for in her waning years gave Xandra an unexpected peek at a new side of him. He suddenly seemed less like a war-hardened bully.

It could be an act, the cynical side of her, created by her brother and Michael, speculated.

"I wish I'd gotten to see Maggie again before she passed away," Adam said, leaning his back against the neighboring stall. Beams of sunlight shone in his honey-colored hair. He sighed and his wide shoulders slumped a bit. "I can't believe I only missed her by two months. She was more of a mother to me than our real mother was. It's hard knowing she never got all the letters I sent to the house for her.''

Beth smiled gently, wistfully, as she laid her hand on Adam's shoulder. "She knew. She was forever telling me not to assume too much about your silence all those years. She suspected they'd destroyed your letters but said she would have been risking her job and losing me if she said or did anything about it. I'm sorry you missed seeing her, but it was bad at the end. This way you have your good memories of Maggie. She's been at peace all these months in a much better place.''

"If you say so," Adam said, looking skeptical.

"I do," Beth told him. "She loved the Lord so much, Adam. She's in heaven. Believe it. I'll get all your stuff together before you leave today. Maybe going over some of the things that were yours when you were his age would help you and Mark relate to each other," Beth suggested as she swatted the shoulder she'd patted so gently not a minute ago. "If you hadn't kept buying Boyerton such a deep dark secret, I could have left it all at the house for you.''

"I just didn't have time to let you know I was trying to buy it before I shipped out. Thanks for rescuing what you did. I owe you one, kiddo.''

"I'll remember you said that. So are you up to a challenge?'' she asked her brother. "Mischief will give you one. And it would be a big help if you'd ride him. Cole's away and—'' she laughed "—Mischief is a bit of a handful.''

"I was just going to hang out and watch Mark.''

"You'll make the kid nervous. Come on. You never forget how to ride. You know that. It'll be fun, I promise."

Adam pushed off the stall and stuffed his hands in the back pockets of his worn jeans. "Maybe it is time. Ross used to let me sneak over here and ride his horse. It was the only time I enjoyed riding, so I guess this is the place to start. So tell me all about this miscreant animal of Cole's."

Beth hooked her arm through the crook of Adam's and pulled him down the aisle. As their footsteps receded, she started telling him the story of how Mischief had once lured her into position and pushed her into a mud puddle.

Xandra stayed right where she was, continuing to pet Fly Boy so he wouldn't draw attention to himself or her hiding place. She would die if Adam realized she'd been too much of a coward to face him.

Her disquiet didn't lessen as Beth got to the punch line of her story and Adam's laughter echoed through the stable; it grew. If he'd been handsome when angry, wary or sad, then relaxed and happy, he was devastating. Devastating to Xandra's peace of mind, anyway.

Because with men, what you saw was *not* what you got. She should know. Her brother had looked like an angel and yet she had spent her childhood being tortured by him. Michael Balfour had seemed like Dr. Jeckyll but had turned into Mr. Hyde soon after their wedding.

What hid behind Adam Boyer's handsome face and

glittering green eyes? And why did she keep wondering?

She leaned her forehead against Fly Boy's, fighting off a sudden feeling of hopelessness and a loneliness so deep it had her blinking back tears. For months on the road knocking around the country on her circuitous route back here, she'd begged the God she remembered little about to deliver her home, to give her peace and strength and a new life. And He had given her all that. So why was she so sad? What was the matter with her? She had the life she'd prayed for. Didn't she?

Adam hitched Mischief to the snubbing post in the yard and waved to Jack. He'd only ridden for an hour, his mind on Mark most of that time.

"How's he doing?" he called to his brother-in-law.

Jack motioned him over to the exercise ring where Mark trotted a palomino. His sister's husband, wearing a white Stetson, work jeans and a tan shearling coat, sat atop the practice ring fence with the heels of his work boots hooked on a lower slat. He looked like something out of the Old West, while he himself looked like a refugee from the armed services. Instead of riding boots, his were ones that had stomped over some of the roughest terrain he'd seen in his nearly twenty years in the Navy. His olive foul-weather jacket had nothing to recommend it save warmth and military efficiency. Adam took a deep breath of clean air that was liberally mixed with the smell of hay and horse and leather. Neither man looked as if he belonged on an eastern horse farm, but Adam thought Jack felt as comfortable there as Adam himself did.

It was good to be home.

He shook himself out of his own introspection when Jack shouted another instruction. Jack seemed to want him to draw his own conclusion. The kid seemed to be doing well. "So he's doing okay," Adam said, interested and hopeful but trying not to care. This was Mark's life, and his interests were his own.

Jack chuckled. "Your kid's a natural. I guess horsemanship really is in the genes. We talked about regular lessons. I hope you don't mind."

"Nah. He looks good up there," he said, admiring Mark's obvious natural aptitude. "If he wants to ride, he can ride. For fun or as a serious pursuit. All I know is, my father won't be involved. As long as you're here, I guess you're elected. What are Laurel Glen's fees?"

Jack shook his head. "No way I'm charging family. How's Sunday for you until Daylight Savings Time gives us longer evenings? Ross doesn't care how I spend my time, but that's my day off. I'd feel better showing Mark the ropes then."

"Anytime should be fine. I put in some time doing talks and such for the local recruiting office, but that's pretty much it. My days aren't exactly full right now."

"Beth can teach him jumping and English tack if he wants," Jack suggested. "Morning handles either, so I put him up in western gear today. It's what I know and I think it's easier to start with.''

Adam leaned his shoulder against the corner of the brick wall of the stable. ''It's all up to Mark. I'm not pushing him either way. I refuse to follow in my father's footsteps... So, have you and Beth made any decisions about staying in the east or going back home?''

''This was only supposed to be temporary for me. I only came to find my mother and get to know her and the family I didn't know I was part of. But now Beth is in my life and she's from the area. Plus my sister married a guy from here and she has no intention of going back to Colorado. Now you've come back and that's another tie for Beth. Frankly, until last night we had more reason to stay than to go.''

''Last night?''

Jack grimaced and glanced around at the heart of Laurel Glen's operation. Adam followed his gaze, taking in two of the four long and low stone and brick stables that formed an X with the practice ring in the center. That was where Mark was making half-circle reverses, leading the horse in what looked like a figure eight.

Adam glanced over his shoulder at an historic octagon-shaped barn nestled in a copse of winter-bare oaks and towering white pines farther up the drive. There were also two small white cottages, one of which currently was home to his sister and Jack. In the distance Laurel House rose from the top of a hill overlooking all of Laurel Glen like an elegant lady surveying her children at play.

"My father called," Jack said at last. "I've forgiven him for lying all those years about my being adopted but…" He shrugged. "What can I say? Things weren't perfect before I found the adoption papers. Dad says he wants to sign the Circle A over to me and my sister. He still wants to live there, but he claims to need to let go of the place emotionally. That makes sense, since he's been seeing a psychologist for over a year about his obsession with the ranch."

"How do you feel about the Circle A?"

"I don't remember when I didn't want to run the operation, but when I was foreman, Dad was constantly looking over my shoulder and second-guessing me." Jack sighed. "He promised it would be hands-off this time. He even promised us the house to ourselves."

"For what it's worth, I think you should give it a try. There's nothing worse than giving up on a dream."

"The way you have by retiring?" Jack asked, then turned away to yell an instruction to Mark, who turned the horse toward the center of the ring, guiding her into a perfect figure eight. Mark beamed with pride when Morning performed as directed. "The kid's hooked," Jack said, then raised an eyebrow.

Adam didn't bother pretending it wasn't a reminder that he hadn't answered Jack's question. "I wasn't thinking about my career. The Navy was good to me.

Being a SEAL was exciting and gratifying, but it isn't the only thing I can do with my life. I was remembering how it felt when Mallory left and I all but lost Mark. I took the easy way out for too long, letting Mallory dictate how much I could see him. Letting Jerry be the father. It's a mistake I'd never repeat. I have a second chance to be a father now and nothing is going to stand in my way.''

"Good attitude. I wish my father had cared as much about us as you do about Mark.''

"Hi, Ms. Lexington,'' Mark shouted. "How was your weekend? I didn't know you come here. I'm going to start taking lessons from my uncle.''

"It looks as if you've taken quickly to riding,'' Alexandra Lexington called back to Mark as she climbed up on the fence across the big practice ring.

She looked around, seeming to scan the area. He wondered if she was making sure he wasn't around.

She needn't have bothered. Adam had no intention of dealing with her a second time in one day. He was sure by her relaxed manner that she hadn't seen him standing down on the ground next to Jack. He stepped farther into the shadows, hoping to keep it that way.

"How was Fly Boy today?'' Jack called to her.

Adam winced and held his breath. Would she see him hiding like the coward he was?

"He was a perfect gentleman,'' she yelled back, laughter in her voice.

"Mark, I think you've had enough. Dismount and walk him around the ring a bit to cool him down,'' Jack said as he hooked a leg over the top of the tall fence. "Remember to keep the reins in your hand so neither one of you can step on them, and keep your feet under you, not him." Jack looked back down at Adam. "You need help putting Mischief away?" he asked, clearly puzzled when he saw Adam almost cowering by the stable.

"No problem," Adam answered. After Jack nodded and jumped to the ground inside the ring, Adam turned away and sighed. It looked as if Murphy's Law was at work in his life again. Every time he drove Mark over here for a lesson, he'd run the risk of seeing her.

And something else. He couldn't understand Jack being so nice to a member of the family who'd been so cruel to Beth all these years. Of course, Laurel Glen was a business, and Jack was technically an employee, but the Taggerts saw both him and Beth as family. Why would any of them be willing to deal with a Lexington?

He was going to have to ask Beth. He saw no other way around it. He'd hesitated to even mention it, worried about bringing up such a painful subject. Especially when he felt so guilty for not being there for her all those years ago when she'd needed him.

When Mark was ready to leave, the day that had gone from bad to worse continued to go downhill. All the way home, his son regaled him with more of his unending praise of the wonderful, perfect, unequaled Ms. Alexandra Lexington.

Chapter Eight

Early on Monday afternoon Xandra practically flew up Laurel Glen's drive on the way to Jack Alton's office. He'd called her at work just as she was packing up to leave for the day. After a little over two weeks of searching, he'd located a horse he thought might be perfect for her. The only catch was that she had to move quickly, because the quarter horse looked like a real prize.

She was in such a rush she nearly passed Fly Boy's stall without stopping to pet him. But the affable quarter horse trumpeted an insistent greeting, and she froze in her tracks in the aisle. "Oh, sorry, pal. I'm not very loyal, am I." She blew in his nostrils, saying hello in horse language, and rubbed his velvet nose, then all was forgiven. "I'll be back to see you later. I promise."

"Oh, for goodness' sake, dear, don't let this trickster fool you," Meg Taggert drawled as she sauntered up behind Xandra to rub Fly Boy's forehead. "He just had an apple and a lump of sugar from me not two minutes ago."

Xandra had always admired Meg. Now in her early fifties, she was a startling sight with her youthful face, dark arched eyebrows and snow-white cap of hair. She was dressed for riding in a classic competition-style jacket, suede jodhpurs, shining leather boots and a velvet helmet. Her only concession to the cold was a heavy turtleneck sweater and gloves.

While Xandra felt a bit underdressed in her ski jacket and jeans, she knew Meg Taggert wouldn't judge her. She never valued anyone by anything but their heart. She'd once overheard Meg deal her mother quite a set down on the subject at a charity ball. As muddle-headed as she had been that particular night, it had been all Xandra could do not to cheer. She liked to think she'd come so far that these days she might deliver the lecture herself.

"Hello, Ms. Taggert." She greeted Meg with a wide smile. "Did you have a good time on your trip? I hope you don't mind that Beth let me ride Fly Boy while you were gone."

"No thanks are necessary. I heard you and my big boy here became fast friends while I was floating on the Caribbean. He needed the exercise. You're welcome to ride him anytime. And please call me Meg. 'Ms. Taggert' makes me feel so old."

Xandra chuckled. "You'll never be old. Old is a state of mind. And thanks for the offer to ride Fly Boy but it may not be necessary. Jack called, and he may have found a horse for me. He has a video stream for me to look at. I hope it works out.''

''Is that where you were off to in such a rush that you nearly ignored my Fly Boy? If my son likes this animal, you can bet he's good horseflesh.'' Companionably she looped an arm over Xandra's shoulders. ''Let's go take a look at this wonder.''

They walked down the shadowed, musky aisle toward the foreman's office. It was paneled in rich old knotty pine, and the smell of the wood fire flickering in the cast-iron stove in the far corner flowed around them. Meg pushed her ahead, and she noticed Beth curled up on the worn hunter-green leather sofa with a woolen blanket tossed over her legs.

''Mom!'' Jack called out, and jumped to his feet behind his desk to give his mother a kiss on the cheek.

Beth looked up and grinned. ''Wait till you see this character, Xandra. There's no way you aren't going to want a closer look at him. I *have* a horse and I still want this guy.''

''This fellow is at the top of your price range but he comes with his own western tack,'' Jack said, and waved Xandra behind his old scarred wooden desk and settled her into his chair. He leaned over her to punch keys and click the mouse.

''Fifteen-and-a-half hands high,'' Jack continued, absently cataloguing the attributes of his find as he navigated the computer. ''He's dark brown with a black mane and tail. No other markings.''

Anticipation built until Xandra was hardly able to

stay in the chair. "I feel like it's Christmas and I'm six again!" she said.

Jack, Beth and Meg all laughed.

"He's a nice-looking animal," Jack went on, "and he's cross-trained in eventing and barrel racing of all things. Jennifer, the owner, didn't know what she wanted to compete in, so her father decided on a quarter horse since they're accepted in both arenas of competition. Which is perfect, since you mentioned liking Fly Boy's western gear."

"Why are they selling him? Oh," Xandra said, not waiting for an answer and falling instantly in love as the video splashed onto the screen. "He's gorgeous."

Jack chuckled. "They got the name right, that's for sure. Dauntless. Look at this guy, Mom."

They all crowded behind the desk then, watching Dauntless fill the computer monitor. With his head held at a perfect forty-five-degree angle, he pranced around a ring, his carriage vaunting his own high opinion of himself.

Then there was a scene switch, and he stood as still as a statue in the center of a competition ring with a pretty teenage girl on his back. Suddenly, his rider gave him a subtle signal, and he wheeled around keeping his rear legs in place. Then horse and rider took to the air, flying over a series of jumps.

Xandra stood transfixed as the video blinked to yet a different scene. The girl, dressed now like a cowgirl, pointed Dauntless toward a line of barrels. Xandra had never seen anything like the way the five-year-old gelding cut in and out of the barrels in a series of tight turns and then skidded to a dead stop before the judges.

Next they were back at the first location—what looked like a private stable yard—to show off a few tricks. Xandra's favorites were Dauntless counting off his age with his hoof and his last, making a bow and then using his teeth to doff the girl's hat. As the video faded out, Dauntless bent his head over his knees to farther deepen the bow, the hat still dangling from his teeth.

Utterly charmed, Xandra covered her heart with her hand and told them, "I don't care why they're selling him. I want him."

Jack laughed. "Not so fast. You need to take a closer look at him. You can't judge him from what you can see on a video. He looks good. Smart as a whip and good-natured. I doubt there's anything wrong with him but rein in that enthusiasm a little. Besides, remember I mentioned that you have to go meet Jennifer? That was her riding him. She insists on meeting the person who wants to buy him before she'll approve the sale. And I'll warn you, so far she's turned down three offers."

"Actually, I think I like her for that. So, just out of curiosity…"

"Why are they selling him?" Jack put in with a wide smile.

"Jennifer decided on eventing and Dauntless isn't doing well at dressage. If she keeps him as a pleasure horse, Dauntless would spend an awful lot of time not being ridden, and she doesn't want to do that to him.

They live in Maryland, near D.C. You willing to make the trip to see him?''

Xandra nodded. ''Make the arrangements. I can go any day this week after noon because of teacher conferences. I don't want to chance waiting till next weekend.''

''Whoa. I think you should move on this quickly, too, but I can't go down there at all this week with Ross and Cole both still away. I'm just too backed up.''

Xandra's heart dipped. She looked at Beth, who'd retreated to the sofa. ''Do you know how to tell if he's healthy?''

''Not really.'' Beth blushed a little. ''I'd never even curried Glory until I met Jack. He's been teaching me a lot, but I wouldn't feel confident advising you on something this important.''

''I'm sorry, dear,'' Meg said. ''I'd go, but I promised every afternoon this week to the Historical Society. We're in the middle of setting up for the charity ball and auction this weekend.''

''I've looked through the breeding records on Dauntless,'' Jack said, settling on the edge of the desk, ''and they look good. Still, I think someone knowledgeable should look him over. This is an important purchase. Do you have anyone you could take along who knows horses?''

Deflated, Xandra got up and walked to the opposite end of the old leather sofa from Beth. ''No,'' she said, dropping onto the worn cushion. ''I don't know a soul I could take.''

A car door slammed outside. "I do," Beth said, her eyes brightening. "Hold on a minute." She was on her feet and gone in a blink.

"I think our Beth had a brainstorm," Meg drawled as she settled in the chair behind the desk Xandra had vacated.

Moments later the deep timbre of male voices blending with Beth's made Xandra's stomach do a freefall.

She couldn't.

She *wouldn't*.

"Jack's got a line on a great quarter horse for Xandra," Beth was telling her brother when they entered the office together.

Adam's presence seemed to suck every cubic inch of air from the room and the small, cozy office turned claustrophobic. Beth, however, didn't seem to notice the loss of all available breathing room. Instead she rushed ahead with her explanation, leaving Xandra tongue-tied and aghast at the way her lovely day had fallen apart.

"Could you look him over with her?" Beth asked finally.

"I've got the time, but who's Xandra?" Adam answered.

When he followed Beth's gaze to the old sofa, it was clear he hadn't noticed Xandra sitting there. Noah Webster could have used Adam's picture as an illustration next to several words: *stunned, poleaxed, stupefied.* They all fit. Were she not in this awful, awkward situation with him, Xandra would have had a good laugh at his expense. But she was in the same soup, and it was no fun at all.

"No, Beth," she said quickly, scooting to the edge of the cushion and trying her best to glare surreptitiously at her friend. "I'll be fine. I wouldn't think of imposing on your brother."

"But you won't be. *I* will," Beth countered, unaccountably blind to Xandra's signals. "I'm the one who asked."

"But you asked for me. And really, I can handle it on my own. Besides, you told me it had been years since your brother has been around horses."

"Adam knew more about horses at fifteen than the average rider ever learns. Tell her, Adam. I don't want her to chance losing Dauntless by waiting till next weekend."

"Nice of you two to remember I'm standing here," he said, looking grumpy and bewildered at once. "I need something cleared up for me. It's had me puzzled. From what I'd heard our families rival the Montagues and the Capulets. Which should make you two archenemies. Now I walk in on this cozy scene. I'm a little more than slightly confused."

"Enemies? Xandra and me? Where would you get such a ridiculous idea?" Beth demanded.

Xandra could well imagine—her mother!

Adam frowned, looking uncomfortable. "I'm not sure. I must have misinterpreted something someone, er, said," he explained, a mile-wide streak of gallantry showing itself and endearing him to Xandra for once.

With the exception of Beth, it had been years since anyone protected her. In fact, no one until Beth ever really had.

"Probably my mother," Xandra put in.

"That woman!" Meg all but growled as she scooped up a pile of papers from Jack's desk and tapped them into an orderly stack. Even though she was uncomfortable, Xandra found Jack's horrified expression funny.

Beth huffed out a breath that sounded tired and nearly defeated. "Adam, I recommended Xandra for her job at the school. Would I do that for an enemy? You don't want people judging you by our parents, do you?"

Adam grinned, his gaze ensnaring her own. "I believe someone else already said exactly that to me, but I didn't have all the facts. I'm sorry I've misjudged you, Ms. Lexington."

He looked at his sister, and Xandra was able to take a breath. Beth, she realized, hadn't mention her involvement at New Life, and Xandra was relieved. But she was also sorry because she couldn't help wondering what he'd think if he learned what a coward she'd been to allow Michael to abuse her.

"Beth, if you can pick up Mark after school tomorrow," Adam was saying, "and let him stay here with you till we get home, I'd be glad to drive…Xandra…to Maryland."

Xandra stood. "I…no, really."

"Let me do this. It's the least I can do after giving you such a rough time."

"You have nothing to make up for. This is just too much to ask even if you are my friend's brother. I can go alone," she protested.

"Why not go for a ride and settle the details between you?" Meg ordered, still straightening Jack's desk. "I have something I want to talk over with Jack and Beth."

"Good idea. With Cole still away, Mischief could use another good workout," Jack said.

"You can trust my brother," Beth whispered for Xandra's ears only, as she dragged her to her feet. "It's time to take another step."

Fine for Beth to say. Buying the horse was supposed to be her next step, not riding with a man. But maybe she could get out of having him accompany her to Maryland by going with him now. That way it would just be the two of them with no Beth, Meg or Jack to throw a spanner into the works. They'd ride together, she'd decline his generous offer and she'd make herself scarce.

Perfect plan.

Adam watched Alexandra and Fly Boy race across the meadow toward him and marveled at the change in her. She had such a beautiful smile. A wonderful laugh. And she loved riding. Not even the cold seemed to affect her; her cheeks were reddened and even her nose was pink. With the temperatures now in the high forties, she probably thought of this as warm weather.

For him this was nothing compared to winter in

some of the places he'd been. Mark, however, reminded him daily that this wasn't what he was used to and he hated it. The teenager spent the entire ride to and from school grousing about the cold and snow. It was better than his previous silence, but tiring all the same.

Adam followed as Alexandra charged up a hill, the horse's hooves pulverizing the thawing ground and splashing mud everywhere. Suddenly he realized that the joy he'd found in secretly riding Ross's horse as a boy had returned, and he was afraid it wasn't because he was at Laurel Glen again.

He wished he could hang back and let Alexandra go off alone. It would make life much easier. Because he knew with a sick certainty that the joy he was feeling came from watching her exuberant happiness.

It was definitely a worry.

But he'd learned a long time ago that avoiding a problem didn't make it go away. It just gave the problem time to get worse. The last two weeks had proven that. He pursed his lips, allowing himself to think about her, and realized she wasn't really the problem at all.

He was lonely. That was it in a nutshell.

And he was very attracted to Alexandra Lexington. She popped into his thoughts constantly.

Until an hour ago he'd thought there were perfectly logical reasons why he had to stay away from her. He had thought she'd been cruel to his sister. But instead it turned out they were friends. He had thought she intended to use Mark somehow. But if she was Beth's friend, then she'd truly been trying to help him, and with the purest of motives—the good of his son. So there was nothing standing in the way of their becoming friends.

"Adam, you're off the hook," Alexandra said when he pulled Mischief to a stop next to her at the summit of the hill. "I'll be careful and check Dauntless's health records. I can go alone."

"Don't be silly. I said I'd go with you."

"No, really. I know you don't want to help me. I accept your apology for misunderstanding my relationship with Beth. But the animosity has been about more than that. You've obviously resented every suggestion I've made where Mark is concerned."

She was right. His apology had been grossly incomplete. "I resented you because you seemed to have all the answers and I was floundering. Please understand, I had no idea what I was walking into when I went to pick him up at his aunt's last month." He sighed and let his chin drop to his chest. "Has it only been a month?"

"And February's a short month." She chuckled and flipped her long hair over her shoulder.

It was the first time he'd seen it down and the way those silken tresses shimmered and floated on the chill breeze was spellbinding.

"But seriously," she was saying, "did you have no warning at all of his resentment?"

Adam forced his mind back on track. "Not a one. His reaction to me had done a complete one-eighty since I'd last seen him. I was floored. We'd always been easy with each other.'' He took off his sunglasses, determined to reach out to her no matter how much the idea scared him. He was trained to laugh death and torture in the face. He could do this. ''And then there you were, days later, telling me I was handling him all wrong.''

''I'm sor—''

''No,'' he interrupted, shaking his head. ''I'm the one who should be sorry. Who *is* sorry. You were only trying to help. Beth called it shooting the messenger. I'm really sorry.''

''You're forgiven,'' she said.

Adam unconsciously sent the horse a confusing signal with his legs. He nearly lost his seat when Mischief sidestepped in confusion. ''That simple? 'You're forgiven'? Even I'm not sure I deserve to get off the hook so easily.''

She seemed to eye him carefully as if weighing whether to wade into dangerous waters.

''Go ahead and say what you're thinking,'' he urged. ''I'm going to prove to you that you don't need to worry that I'll go off again. Really. I'm pretty tame once you get to know me.''

She shot him a look of mixed disbelief and mockery. ''I'm sure you're a real pussycat. So here goes— are you as hard on Mark as you are on yourself?''

He frowned and searched his recent memory. ''No. No, I'm not. I know he's grieving and acting out because of it, so I cut him as much slack as I can without letting him walk all over me.''

She looked down and flicked at a splatter of mud

on her thigh. When she looked back up, the sun sparkled in her eyes. They were more blue than gray today, reflecting the bright sky all around them. "Okay, then," she said with a quick nod. "I said you're forgiven and I meant it. How could I withhold forgiveness from you and profess to be a Christian? After all, Jesus forgave me my sins just for the asking."

Adam stared at her. So far every one of Beth's circle of friends took this Christianity thing so seriously that it never ceased to amaze him. Uncomfortable in the face of her graciousness, he nodded and changed the subject.

"I appreciate your kindness and all you've done for Mark. He's doing great in school." Adam chuckled at the memory of the report card incident. "I hung his report card on the fridge. He said it was 'lame' but it's still there, so I figure I didn't mess up for once. Since then we've had a few lighter moments, but he always seems to pull back and get worse than before for a while. So can we effect a truce between us? I could use a little peace. Maybe working together, we can find out what's up with my son."

"A truce would be good," she said, turning slowly toward him, that wary look still in her eyes.

Adam considered her for a moment. Was she afraid of him? With a pang he remembered Mallory pulling away from him after seeing a documentary on the SEALs. Mark had been three then and it was around the time she'd started getting protective and critical of how he'd played with Mark. But he hadn't been too rough with his son and he wasn't a violent person.

Adam had just decided to ignore the caution in her tone when he had to check Mischief with a tug on the reins to keep him from taking a bite out of Fly Boy's hindquarter. "You know, Horse, I get enough of this kind of grief from my kid. Knock it off," he growled.

Alexandra raised an eyebrow. "You're equating Mark to Mischief? Mischief is legendary around here. And this is *good* behavior from what I hear. He's just testing you a little."

"Yeah, just like Mark spends most of his time at home testing me." Adam paused, sobering as he carefully examined the reins in his hand before looking up. "Tests I'm afraid I keep failing." He looked away, then back again. "Frankly, I need someone to talk with about him or my head's going to explode. I know I can't let him know he's getting to me, but I can't keep bottling up my frustration and I hate unloading on Beth and Jack. They're newlyweds and they have enough pressure right now. Jack's father wants him back home running the Circle A."

"I know. Beth told me. She wants what's best for Jack. He wants what's best for her. I'd miss her, but she might be better off away from my mother and Mother's vicious circle of friends. Beth and Jack are praying about it, so I know they'll do what's right. Any way you look at it, though, it's a big decision. I understand why you don't want to add to their burden. I'll be happy to schedule a meeting whenever you need to talk."

"I'm not sure that would work. I think what you

said about Mark needing you as a confidante was right. He isn't talking to me and he just lost his mother and stepfather. So the more I show up at the school, the bigger chance I have of running into Mark and cutting you off from him. I don't want to risk that.''

Alexandra frowned. "Call me, then.''

"I thought the ride down to see this horse would give us some time to compare notes. I'm worried that he's going to do something foolish. Is there a reason you don't want to accept my help? I didn't think I'd been that obnoxious.''

"No.'' She took a deep breath. "No, you haven't. Okay. I accept your help deciding on Dauntless so we can talk out this problem with Mark.''

He reached out to shake her hand, thinking to seal the deal, but it felt as if he might have sealed his fate instead. Because just as her scent had scrambled his senses that Sunday morning at church, the feel of her small, soft hand sliding into his short-circuited whatever was left of his brain.

What was going on here? This was supposed to be about Mark and maybe building a friendship with another adult. Sure she was a beautiful woman, but beautiful women were plentiful around Coronado and SEALs attracted them like magnets. He'd had a string of casual, short-term relationships over the years. And none of those women had affected him as Alexandra did. What was so different about her?

Chapter Nine

The sky was heavy with what looked like snow the next day when Xandra pulled her car into the small parking area behind Laurel Glen's stables. She refused to let the bleak skies affect her mood in spite of her misgivings about the upcoming ride.

When Adam had confessed that he wasn't dying to run into her mother again, she suggested they meet at Laurel Glen. Everyone assumed she lived with her parents and she didn't correct the assumption. Giving out her address at New Life Inn wasn't allowed since keeping the whereabouts of the shelter confidential was paramount.

But if Xandra was honest with herself, as her therapist insisted she be, then she had to admit she didn't want Adam or anyone else to know about her connection to New Life, lest it lead to a discussion of her marriage and divorce. Though she was working on it, Xandra hadn't yet gotten past the shame. She was afraid people would think she was weak and cowardly for allowing herself to be victimized by her ex-husband.

But she wasn't weak, she told herself. Not anymore. She'd stayed on at New Life to relieve Beth at nights, not because she couldn't live on her own. She was there so she'd be available to other women like herself during the dark hours of the night. Only someone who understood would do for midnight heart-to-hearts when shadows grew threatening.

She sighed. Now if she could only completely convince herself of all that, she'd have conquered Michael and he'd cease to have any control over her.

Determined to face this day as she had all the rest in the difficult journey back from her prison of fear and self-doubt, she got out of her white midsize convertible and looked around. Since hers was the only vehicle in the little gravel lot, Xandra assumed Adam hadn't yet arrived or that he'd parked somewhere near the cottage where Beth and Jack lived.

She was unsure how she felt about having to wait for Adam. Sometimes putting off the inevitable was a blessing, a reprieve. Other times it was a curse that extended the torture of apprehension. As she felt her nerves tightening, she acknowledged that today it was definitely the latter.

She knew that after Jack had made the arrangements for today's meeting, Dauntless's owners had e-mailed detailed directions to him, so Xandra went in search of him. She found him with Adam as soon as she walked around the stable nearest the drive.

They were hitching a trailer to one of Laurel Glen's pickups. She hadn't even thought of transportation except that she'd intended to do the driving so she could concentrate on the road and not the man who would be beside her.

Apparently using her car wasn't in his plan at all.

"Afternoon, Xandra," Jack called to her. "Adam and I got a head start. You two are all set. Good luck." He turned away, waving over his shoulder in his hurry to get back to work.

For a moment she thought Adam had decided to defer. He walked to the passenger side door. All he did, however, was open it, and turn to wait for her to reach him.

"I thought I'd drive," she said, forgetting even to say hello.

Adam blinked, whether at her accidentally sharp tone or the idea of being driven by a woman, she wasn't sure. "U-uh," he stammered, then recovered with a shrug. "Sure. It's just been my experience that most women don't drive stick. Especially a five-speed."

She guessed she was like most women, then. "Oh. It's a manual?" Xandra's heart tripped, fell, then took off running again. It looked like there'd be no distraction from his commanding presence for her today.

"Yeah. Five on the floor."

"I guess you're stuck. Sorry. I thought since this was my trip, I should bear the brunt of the grunt work involved."

"Alexandra, this isn't that big a deal for me. My

work schedule is about as flexible as one can get. And I like driving. It relaxes me. Plus pulling a big trailer can be tricky. It's no problem. Okay?''

She huffed out a breath and willed her speeding heart to slow. "I'm sorry," she said just before he closed her door. "I'm not used to relying on anyone.''

Adam gave her a long assessing look when he climbed in next to her. "And I've lived a life that depends on teamwork. A SEAL relies on his swim buddy and the rest of his team for his life. Maybe we can learn from each other. Now that I don't have anyone to share decisions with.'' He grinned. "I'm like a...seal out of water.''

What an intriguing thought. Could he possibly mean he wasn't used to being in control and he didn't like it now that he was? "What about Mark?" she probed. "Other than the decision to move here, do you talk decisions over with him?''

Adam pursed his lips and carefully shifted into first gear. The trailer jerked just a bit as he started rolling them forward. "You mean like what to order for dinner? Or more on the order of who to hire as help around the house?''

"Both. Everything. Day-to-day life is full of little decisions. The more you share with him—the more control you give him—the more comfortable he's going to be.''

He gave her a sidelong glance. "Why do I get the feeling that you think I'm some kind of control freak? If anything I'm just the opposite. You have no idea how terrified I was moving him here.''

"You spent four-point-two million dollars to move him here. That doesn't sound a bit scared to me. That sounds confident and a little bit arrogant."

"I didn't buy Boyerton to live there."

Her eyes widened. "What?"

Adam's grin was sheepish. "It was a purely emotional decision made about half an hour before I shipped out last year. That's when I got my first letter from Beth. In passing she mentioned that our father was in financial trouble and trying to break up the property to sell to developers. She said she thought it was a spite move against Ross Taggert."

"He and Ross *have* crossed swords over the last few years."

"Well, I was the reason the animosity started. He blamed Ross for my quitting eventing."

"Why would he blame Ross?"

"Some of my few happy memories come from this place," he said just as they passed under Laurel Glen's iron entrance arch and out onto Indian Creek Road. "Ross used to let me sneak over here to ride his horse. Just to ride. No one timing me. No one judging my form or the horse's gait. Father found out. That ended that for me. As far as I knew he never lowered himself to talk to Ross, who was scrabbling to keep Laurel Glen running back then."

"So in a way you felt responsible, somehow."

"Right. When Beth said Father wanted to back a housing development up against Ross's property, I got hold of the guy who handles my investments and told him to buy it. He kept my name out of it, or I'd bet Father would have refused the sale. He thought we were developers.''

"Everyone did. Then the property just sat vacant. I guess you hadn't yet decided to retire.''

Adam shot her an enigmatic look. "If Mark's mother hadn't died, I doubt I ever would have retired. I would probably have visited occasionally and stayed in the carriage house. Maybe left it to Beth and Mark. I doubt I'd ever have gotten Mark here to see Boyerton.''

"So Mark's right that you gave up the SEALs for him.''

He shook his head. "I just gave up one kind of family for another. Unfortunately, this one's favorite word is 'whatever.'''

"Why didn't you think you'd get to bring him here?''

Adam didn't answer. Instead he made a great production of pulling onto the highway off the entrance ramp from the rural road to the interstate. Silence reigned for several minutes, and she let it.

Finally, when she thought she'd have to say something to break the building tension, he sighed. "Mallory purposely got in the way of my visitation. Especially recently. She wanted Jerry to be Mark's father. According to what you've told me, she succeeded, even though I wouldn't let Jerry adopt Mark. She'd been pushing for that for years, but I refused. I doubt he even knows she blocked a lot of my attempts to see him.''

She turned slightly in her seat, trying to gauge his

reaction. "Actually, I think he knew about the visitation problems to some extent. Mark said something to me about it."

Adam's head snapped toward her, a perplexed expression on his face. "Now I'm more confused than ever," he said, then looked back at the road. "If he knows I wanted to see him, if he didn't resent my career, why is he so angry?"

"I guess it's time for me to wear my guidance hat. I'll see what I can find out."

"Good luck. At this point, I'm for anything that'll stop the 'whatever' answers. So, are you going to let Dauntless keep his name?"

Adam sounded tired, and she could see that though their conversation had seemed to flow fairly easily, it had put him through an emotional wringer. Funny, he wasn't at all the kind of man she'd assumed he was. Beth really did appear to know her brother well, in spite of their many years of separation.

There were, of course, physiological theories to support that. It was said that a child's early experience formed a good portion of his personality. So by high school graduation, which was when Beth had last seen her brother, Adam already had become the man he was going to be, Navy and SEAL training notwithstanding.

She'd drawn the same kind of analogy before but had come to a different conclusion. Xandra's brother as a boy had certainly been the person—or monster—he was destined to be. If his own reckless driving hadn't brought about his death, she had little doubt he'd be behind bars now and that some poor unfortunate woman would have been his victim.

She glanced at Adam. Something told her Adam Boyer would move heaven and earth to keep from victimizing anyone. She sighed. Of course, she'd thought Michael was her brother's complete opposite at one time, as well. Would she ever reach the point Beth had? Would she ever be able to trust her own judgment again?

Jennifer, the teen who owned Dauntless, okayed Alexandra for the purchase within minutes of meeting her. It stung Adam's conscience that a fourteen-year-old girl had instantly seen who Alexandra was and had displayed better discernment than he himself had. He was incredibly annoyed with himself for having treated her so badly at first.

He patted Dauntless on the neck as he went over the quarter horse. Moving from nose to tail, he mentally checked off every trait Jack had told him to look for. He also eliminated all the usual chronic health problems the magnificent animal's amiable nature might hide. He'd buy the horse himself if Alexandra wasn't already petting and gushing over him.

Adam grinned and looked up, his eyes meeting her anxious ones immediately. "He's in great shape, Alexandra. I'd say you found yourself a new pal."

"You hear that, Dauntless? You're going to have a new home and I'm going to ride you every chance I get. Wait till you see how beautiful Laurel Glen is."

She hugged the big lug around the neck and he just ate it up.

Adam grinned. These two were going to be a real pair. If it wasn't against the law she'd probably want to ride home in the trailer instead of the truck.

An hour later they hit the road with Alexandra sitting in the seat to his right, wiping tears off her cheeks, her scent once again filling the cab.

"I feel so guilty," she sniffled. "Poor Jennifer. She was so upset to see him go."

Adam pressed a handkerchief into her hand. "It was nice of you to tell her she'd be welcome to visit."

"I couldn't do anything else. I hoped giving him up would be a little more bearable for her if it wasn't so final. I know I wish I could visit Rain."

"You can't?"

"He was old and he didn't take to the move. He died. I—I still feel so guilty thinking it was of a broken heart because he missed me."

"You did what you thought was right for him. Right?"

She nodded. Her eyes were dry now but she didn't look convinced. Then in a flash she looked angry. He guessed she was thinking about her marriage and divorce and that the sale of her beloved horse hadn't been necessary since her marriage failed. It was funny, he knew she'd been married briefly but he couldn't understand what kind of man would let a woman like Alexandra Lexington get away. Or do something to make her want to leave.

He stopped himself from asking, and remembered

his own divorce. He'd said a little too much to her on that subject already. He didn't need to confirm what she'd probably guessed—that he'd still been hopelessly in love with his wife when she left.

It was embarrassing how much he'd continued to love Mallory even after that. Helplessly. Stupidly. For years. Actually, until word had come that she was dead. Then sitting in a crude camp overseas, he'd faced the truth about her. He'd spent the following six weeks of his deployment reexamining the previous ten years. Rather than becoming a saint upon her death, Mallory had emerged with all her faults showing.

It had been rough, battling inner demons while fighting a dangerous and cunning foe. He'd come home drained, only to face Mark's new attitude toward him. Still, having Mark back in his life had let Adam begin to heal. He *was* healing. And at a surprising rate, in spite of the problems with his relationship with his son. Maybe because Mallory had been gone from his life for so long.

"Where did you live in California?" Adam asked, searching for a conversation centered on her.

He glanced at Alexandra and noticed her plucking at a loose thread on the seat cushion. "In the northern part of the state. Summit Falls."

"Pretty area."

"It was a world away from Coronado, I'll bet. Mark lived in New Mexico until his mother's death, I take it?"

"Yep," he said. He didn't know enough about his son's life there to comment.

"So how did the Beechams drown?"

Adam massaged a tight muscle in the back of his neck. How did they get talking about him and Mark again? "From what her sister said when she wrote me, it was a second honeymoon. But they didn't really drown. Their boat was cut in half by some drunk in a speedboat. They were both killed on impact."

"That's so sad. Was she a Christian? From something Mark said I gather she might have been."

He shrugged. He didn't really want to talk about Mallory with Alexandra and he refused to examine why. "What difference does it make?"

"For Mark. It might help him if he could be reasonably sure they're in heaven."

Now, that idea really ticked him off and he said so, instinctively, without any thought at all. Then he noticed that she looked so shocked, he might just as well have said he was glad they were dead. Which he wasn't. He'd loved Mallory. And Jerry hadn't been a bad guy. He'd been good to Mark and that said something about the man.

"She really hurt you badly, didn't she," Alexandra said, her expression grave as she reached out and touched his arm.

He told her then. It just all spilled out the way it had started to that day in her office. Maybe it was her touch short-circuiting his brain again. He didn't know why he did it but he told her about the day he'd been wounded. About his battlefield decision to quit the

SEAL teams for Mallory's sake and their son's. About returning home to that letter and finding himself recuperating in an empty house. His years of loving the woman who'd left him without warning. The continued hurt when she'd circumvented his visitation and asked him to give up his rights to Mark altogether. And then the biggest confession of all. He told her why Mallory had tried so hard to keep them apart. She'd said he would be a bad father—as his own had been. And finally he confessed his own fear that she'd been right, though for reasons other than Mallory's.

All the while she just listened, saying nothing. Maybe because he didn't give her a chance to get in a word. Maybe because she was in shock. Maybe because there was nothing to say. Then she said the one thing Mallory never had.

"I'm so sorry."

Chapter Ten

The kindness and sincerity of Alexandra's sympathy jolted Adam, making him realize how much he'd unloaded on her. He swore and smacked the steering wheel. Luckily they were at a red light—one he didn't even remember stopping for.

He looked around. How far had he driven while his mouth went off at a hundred miles per hour? "I'm the one who's sorry. I asked you to be a sounding board about Mark, not about his mother and our sorry relationship."

Her back pressed up against the door, she stared at him, something wary in her expression that he'd seen before but couldn't fully identify. "You…seem to, uh, have a right to your anger," she said so hesitantly it brought him up short.

He'd told her she could say anything she felt he needed to hear. Why was she so nervous? Like Mallory, did she think his being a SEAL labeled him as violent? She was so fair-minded that he just couldn't see her making a snap judgment like that.

"I think I've kept it hidden from Mark. I hope so, anyway." he added, cautiously watching her every reaction. She was becoming quite a puzzle.

"Do you ever force the issue and try to get him to talk about her?"

He stared back, trying to put his finger on what was off-kilter about her reactions. But a horn behind them blared, startling them both. Embarrassed to have forgotten where they were, Adam felt his face heat. He was thankful for the semidarkness left by the setting sun, when he let the clutch up and started them moving forward through the intersection. As if it were a lifeline, he grasped on to the safer subject of Mark. He'd said more than enough about himself, thank you very much.

"The day before I first took him to church, I got Mark to tell me what they did as a family. It wasn't easy, and it hurt to have to ask about how my son had spent his everyday life. I was glad I did it, though, because that's what gave me the idea to take him to church. He was a little ambivalent about the idea. He sounded a little—I guess you could call it—mad at God over her death. At least that's what I got from what he said. But now he seems to enjoy it there, so maybe I'm wrong."

"And what about you? Do you enjoy it?"

He glanced at her and shrugged, tension zinging along his nerve endings. Both felt like loaded questions. "It's a way to get Mark together with some nice kids. Jim Dillon's a good speaker. Even entertaining at times.'' He shrugged, striving for nonchalance. "Other than that, I don't get it. Especially that whole thing he talked about at the end of last week's service. Tell God you believe in Jesus and that you're sorry for your sins and you get a free pass into heaven.''

"It isn't free at all. The whole basis of the Christian faith is that Christ died for our sins. It was a huge payment from a sinless man who was also God incarnate.''

He grinned and shook his head. "I know all that. I'm not a heathen, you know.''

She didn't even chuckle. She merely sat in telling silence for a long, uneasy moment.

"But do you really understand?'' she finally asked. "For instance, if Mallory accepted the salvation offered by Christ's sacrifice on the cross, then she was forgiven by God, even if you haven't forgiven her. Christians are on a path trying to be as perfect as our Savior, but we all fall short. Jesus was the only one who lived a sinless, blameless life.''

He squinted and gave her a quick look. "So you're saying it's okay to hurt people as long as you've said some magic prayer at one point in your life? That just doesn't sound fair. Mallory slept with that man when she was married to me—when I was off getting myself shot to keep her and our country safe. Then she left me for him and took off with my son.''

"Now I'm going to annoy you even more.'' She twisted in her seat, ignoring the constraints of her seat belt. "You're still angry at her. You have to forgive her, Adam. It isn't good to harbor the kind of anger you're feeling for her right now."

He gave her a long look this time before dragging his gaze back to the long ribbon of highway ahead. He had to fight to keep his hands from gripping the wheel too tightly. "Forgive her? How? I know it's been ten years, but I live with Mark. Day in and day out his attitude reminds me that my son is a near stranger because of what they did."

"You don't *try* to forgive people. You *decide* to forgive."

"Decide to?"

"I read that when soldiers are trained in survival they're taught to force themselves to eat something unappetizing by visualizing it as choosing life over death. Have you done that?"

"Tell myself it's for my survival? Yeah. A time or two."

"Forgiveness can be just as important. Anger and hatred eat at us and use up incredible amounts of energy. They fill our souls and keep us from feeling the good things in life. They hold us in the past and stop us from moving ahead, just as effectively as hunger could make a soldier too weak to get back home to safety."

Adam could understand the concept, but right then it didn't seem possible. "You're divorced. Have *you* forgiven *him?*"

Xandra stared at Adam. Was he only turning the

tables on her or did he know the reasons for her divorce? Did he know about the abuse or the infidelity?

The truth was, she *had* forgiven Michael. She had forgiven him for all of it. But it hadn't been easy. Because to grant forgiveness she had had to get angry in the first place. She had fled her marriage in fear, not fury.

Feeling anger was something her therapist had helped her with. Xandra had come to realize that during her marriage she'd turned off her anger response as a safety measure. When Michael had said or done something that would anger any normal red-blooded woman, she'd passively accepted it. It was safer that way. To do otherwise was to give him a reason to retaliate either emotionally or physically. The dawning of her anger had been another step in the right direction.

Forgiveness had been the next.

Xandra paused in self-reflection. It was impossible to miss certain basic similarities between her story and Adam's. Mallory's claim that Adam was a bad father sounded like the same kind of emotional abuse she'd lived with day in and day out. He'd also been cheated on by his wife, as Michael had cheated on her. And Adam had buried his anger behind layers of hurt and self-doubt. Even their distant pasts had a similarity in their upbringing in homes where love had carried conditions.

She couldn't let what Michael had done to her, and her own apprehension about Adam's growing appeal for her, stop her from comforting him. She glanced at him and his gaze flicked her way at the same moment. Their eyes locked.

"I forgave him," she said. "It wasn't easy, but I refused to give him the power to hurt me any longer. I can't pretend to know how much your ex-wife hurt you by taking Mark away, but I do know what it feels like when a spouse is unfaithful."

"The man was an idiot," Adam said baldly, and glanced at the clock on the dashboard. "There's a fast-food place coming up on the right. You want me to stop? We could grab something and eat in the truck if you're hungry."

Her stomach growled. Her hand on her noisy abdomen, she let out an unladylike snort, then slapped her other hand over her mouth to cover a nervous giggle. She knew it had more to do with a sudden relieving of the charged atmosphere than anything else.

"Not the smoothest change of subject I've ever heard," she quipped, smiling to take the sting out of her accusation, "but a pretty effective one. Stop, please. I'm starving."

He grinned and shot her a wry look. "You don't say. I'd never have guessed."

Mark knelt in front of the box of his father's belongings that had just been delivered. He'd decided to carry it upstairs but had accidentally dropped it, and he was checking the damage. Inside, his parents' wedding photo lay on top in a broken frame. They stood in their wedding clothes—his mother in a white gown and his father in dress whites—beneath an arch of crossed swords.

He hadn't thought his father would keep something so sentimental. Feeling responsible, Mark picked the photo up to see if the backing could be fixed...and a letter fluttered out.

He wouldn't have considered reading it but the letter was in his mother's handwriting. His heart squeezed painfully. The letter was short. Mean. Full of truths he'd never understood, and full of lies.

She'd left his father for Jerry, who she said was everything his father wasn't. Mark thought back and remembered coming home from kindergarten and finding Jerry and his mom laughing in the kitchen. Mark had liked Jerry right off because he made his mom laugh more. She had never laughed when his dad was there. When his dad was home they fought sometimes, and Mark had always felt guilty when it happened. So he'd thought Jerry was okay.

But his dad had been okay, too. It had been Mom who was always yelling. Usually when he and Dad were playing.

Mark remembered the report card ceremony now— his dad pinning a ribbon on him for each report card after hanging it on the fridge. He remembered ordinary days when his dad came home and tossed Mark high in the air. Once again, he remembered how his mother would shout that Mark would get hurt, even though his father had never dropped him. So Dad would put him down, smiling but looking kind of worried. Mark had hated that worried sad smile, and so he'd tackle his big, tall father and knock him down. They'd roll around on the ground and laugh. Together.

He smiled sadly, knowing now that he hadn't knocked that big man off his feet at all. Then one day his dad, his hero, had left with his big green pack after promising to be back. But he hadn't come back. The day came when Jerry—he was there all the time by then—had loaded up their things in his car and taken them to New Mexico. His mother had explained that Jerry was his father now and that his dad wasn't ever coming home.

It was all so clear now. And Mark understood. He'd missed more than his bedroom. More than the wallpaper. Had he really told that to this man whom he'd once idolized? He'd missed the bedtime stories his dad used to tell. And the wrestling matches on the floor. The report card ceremonies and those cool ribbons that Mark now recognized as uniform ribbons that represented his father's decorations. Mark had missed a lifetime with his father. His hero.

"Mark?" Adam said from the doorway of his bathroom.

Mark surreptitiously wiped his eyes before turning around and looking up. "Your, uh, your stuff got here," Mark said. He had to get the picture fixed. He couldn't embarrass his father by letting him know Mark had seen that letter. And he had to call Aunt Sky. Maybe he was wrong. Maybe he had the timing wrong in his head. It had been wrong for years, after all. Aunt Sky would know.

Adam, towel around his waist, walked over and looked down at the box. He chuckled. "Yeah. Military efficiency. Apparently there's a town in England with the same name as this one. That's where my stuff was. Thanks for carrying it up."

"Sure," Mark said, and watched his father's face as his gaze came to rest on the wedding picture.

"Man, we were so young," his father said with kind of a sad smile. "We thought we knew it all. Do yourself a favor, son. Don't push growing up too fast. Once you get there, there's no going back."

As Mark let his eyes drop to the picture, he noticed the scar on his father's leg, and something occurred to him that he remembered questioning once before. The leg wound his father had gotten his Purple Heart for. When had it happened?

It was there on their first trip to Disney together, red and angry looking. That's when Mark had asked about the wound, and Adam had brushed it off as unimportant. But the fact was, it had to have been a new wound, or Mark wouldn't have been asking about it.

"Can I look through this stuff?" he asked his father. "It just looks like pictures and commendations. Stuff like that."

Adam shrugged. "Sure. I didn't think you were interested in all that stuff."

Mark shrugged, trying for a neutral expression. "It looks sort of cool."

"Okay, then," Adam said, and just stood there as if he didn't know what to make of Mark being nice.

How wrong was *that?*

"Sully said dinner at seven, though. Try not to be late. He gets cranky when his dinner gets cold before we eat it."

"How can you tell if he *gets* cranky? Seems he's *always* cranky," Mark said, but he smiled. Sully was okay. He even took out the garbage.

Adam smiled, too. "That's Sully. Equal opportunity grump. Then you like him okay? You didn't have an opinion before I called him about the job. How about now?"

Mark stared at his father. He'd said he didn't care. Why did he have to keep rubbing it in? Talk about twisting the knife! "Like I said. *Whatever.* A guy maid is a little weird, but as long as I don't have to call you Commander the way he does, it's all good."

All he got in response was this intense stare. Then his father said, "*Dad* is all I ever wanted to be to you, son."

The sincerity ringing in his voice tossed salt on the wound. Now if Mark could just remember who had made that wound in the first place, maybe he'd understand all this anger he felt.

"Yeah. I think I'm getting that," Mark grumbled, and walked out carrying the box.

He went to his room, determined to find the Purple Heart commendation, call Aunt Sky and piece the truth together. He needed to know. Had his father left them as his mother had said, or had he been deployed? And was he off getting wounded when she'd packed them up and left with Jerry?

He needed the truth no matter how much it hurt, because every day that went by prolonged his father's pain. And as he once again looked down at his mother's letter, Mark had a feeling his father had suffered more than his share already.

Chapter Eleven

Xandra looked up surprised to see Mark Boyer standing hesitantly in her doorway. It was Friday, two days after she and Adam had shared the three-hundred-mile round trip to Maryland, and one fast-food meal.

Closing the file on her desk, she asked, "What's up, Mark?"

"You got a minute?" the youth asked. Mark looked more troubled than usual, making Xandra's heart fall. She had hoped that by now they would have settled in a little better.

"My time is yours, as long as you show me a hall pass. Where are you supposed to be right now?"

"Study hall," he said, and handed her the pass.

She realized what was different about him. His T-shirt was just as big as usual, but his jeans actually fit. Maybe riding was having some effect after all. "In that case, grab a chair. What can I do for you?"

"Some stuff's come up." Mark shrugged. "Plus I've been thinking about something Pastor Jim said last week. I thought maybe you could…you know, help me get my head straight."

"I can certainly try. I'm glad you came to me."

"Yeah. Dad said a smart man learns from his mistakes. I'm thinking he meant that talking is better than doing something stupid again. Right?"

Xandra grinned. "I'd say you learn quickly. Now, what has you upset?"

"I loved my mom. And Jerry. We all got baptized together. So I know they're in heaven now."

So they were covering Sunday's sermon first. If she had to bet, she'd say the "stuff" that had come up was the real reason he'd come to see her. "I imagine that's a great comfort to you. It's funny. Your father and I talked about that sermon on Wednesday."

Mark's eyebrows dipped and his lips pulled together in a frown. "He said Aunt Beth asked him to help you buy a horse."

"Your uncle Jack didn't have time to look Dauntless over, so your father helped. It was very nice of him. Have you talked about your feelings with your father? I know he'd like to help you any way he can."

"I can't talk to him about this."

"But you can. He's your father. You can share anything with him. I don't think I'm wrong about that."

"No. You don't get it. She was so mean to him, Ms. Lexington. And she got me to help. I'm just so mad at her now."

"Are you talking about your mother? I thought it was your father you were angry with."

"I don't know who I'm mad at anymore!" Mark said a bit too loudly. He gripped his thighs, his hands flexing in agitation.

Two students walking down the hall looked toward her office.

"Just talk to me and maybe we can figure it out," she said in an even quieter tone of voice, hoping to calm him, hoping to calm herself. His outburst had taken her by surprise. "That's why I'm here," she went on, proud that she sounded unruffled. "Let's take a walk around the grounds. It's too nice a day to be in this tiny little room."

It was in the sixties and sunny—the spring that had just begun was in the air. They reached the courtyard in the center of the building and she pointed to a bench. "Let's sit." When they'd both settled, she asked, "So what's up?"

Mark took a deep breath. "When I was staying with Aunt Sky after the accident, Dad called to tell me we were moving here and that he was retiring. Mom had been dead for three months and he hadn't called or even written. He wasn't around at all for more than a year. And even before that, he sure never fought back when Mom made up excuses to cancel his visitation. And there he was, out of the blue, expecting me to be grateful or something. I was so mad when he wouldn't let me stay with Aunt Sky."

Mark raked his fingers through his hair, then slumped down on the bench. He looked ready to explode and to cry at the same time. And all of this, save a few details, were facts she already knew.

Give me the right words, Lord. And tell me what he's trying to say. Is he really still angry at Adam over the past?

"But I thought he'd explained that he couldn't be reached. That he called as soon as he was able. Haven't you figured out how much having you with him means to your father?"

Mark's expression turned bitter and his voice rose. "I'm not dumb. I also know what they did. I'm not a little kid anymore, either. I was blind and stupid for listening to their lies. Last night I found the letter she wrote him. She was mean and cruel. Do you know she said he was a bad influence on me? That he was going to turn me into a killer like him? He was a hero, not a killer!"

"Sometimes mothers are too protective of their children."

"Don't defend her," Mark snapped. "Like I said, I found the letter she left him. Jerry, the man I loved instead of Dad, cheated with her. Then he took us to New Mexico to live near his family. Now I remember Jerry from way before we left. He was always around and I wasn't allowed to talk about him with Dad. They got me to help them. I helped break my dad's heart."

Mark sat up, tears running down his face. He wiped them away in an angry gesture. "They lied. They said he left us. But he didn't. He was deployed! He got shot and came home to an empty house and a lousy letter.''

"I know. He told me."

Mark sucked in a shocked breath, a look of surprise and something else in his eyes, then he went on. "No wonder my dad never got married again. No wonder he dates so many women and never marries them. They did that to him."

This was the second time Mark had mentioned Adam and his score of women. It was incredible what a huge impression just seeing a single parent with a potential mate had on children.

"And how do you feel about what your mother did still affecting your father badly?"

"It makes me mad and so sorry that I cried for Jerry. And her. And now Pastor Jim says they're in heaven."

"They're forgiven, Mark. Apparently they realized they'd done wrong and repented. They gave you a good life. Different from the one you would have had with your father in it every day, but you told me it was a good one. And your father has had a very full life doing something he enjoyed."

"And now he's stuck with me. He's living in a house I can see he hates, and he had to give up being a SEAL. For me! And I helped them. I've been so rotten to him since he came to get me. I feel so bad but angry at all of them. And what's worse, I still miss Mom and Jerry. I'm such a terrible person."

"Mark, you are not a terrible person."

"How can Dad still love me after the way I've

treated him? And how's he going to feel when he finds out I helped them?''

Turning toward her Mark pushed his back up against the arm at the end of the bench and pulled his feet up onto the seat, then dropped his head onto his bent knees. He seemed to hide in plain sight. She wondered if he hid from the pain of betrayal, the embarrassment of his tears, or the turmoil in his life. After a moment's thought, she decided it was probably all three.

What people do to their children, Lord! How can I dry his tears of guilt, grief and anger forever? How do I help heal the hurt in his heart? How do I help him begin a good relationship with his father and You when adults have lied to him and taught him to lie for them?

''So let's catalog this,'' she suggested after a moment's thought. ''You're angry at your mother and your stepfather for the way they became a couple. And you're angry at yourself for the grief you feel over their deaths and because you were happy all those years.''

Mark nodded.

''But you're also angry at your father for not leaving you with your aunt, so he could stay in the SEALs. And for not fighting harder to remain in your life all along.''

''Exactly.'' It was clearly a lightbulb moment for Mark. ''My life is so messed up! Nothing makes any sense.''

Xandra put her hand on his head. "Mark, look at me," she ordered.

Mark raised red-rimmed eyes, eyes so like his father's.

"If that's how you're feeling, we'd better restore a little order and reason, hadn't we? The first thing you have to do is identify your feelings. You've said you believe your mother is in heaven. How does that make you feel?"

"H-happy, I guess," Mark stammered. "But I miss her, too."

"Then feel free to grieve. You miss them, and that's okay. You also have to forgive them for making you lie for them and help them cover up their affair. Then forgive yourself."

Mark stared up at her, looking wary. "What about my dad?"

"You need to tell him."

Shaking his head, Mark dropped his forehead back to his knees. "I can't. I know I should admit what I did. But don't you see? My dad is the most honorable person I think I've ever met. How do I tell him what a bad person I am? He gave up everything for me."

"First of all, you are *not* a bad person. A bad person wouldn't be this upset. And you can tell him because he loves you enough to forgive you. Come on. Let's finish this walk. Now I know where we need to go." She stood and urged him to his feet with a hand on his back. When she looked up at his face, she remembered he had inches on her. This boy, whose tears broke her heart and who was in such pain, would be a man very soon. And it was her job to help him become a whole one.

Xandra led the way in silence to a fence that bordered the loading area of the elementary school next door. The kindergarten was just letting out. She smiled at the cute little ones skipping along, dragging their mostly empty backpacks behind them on the ground. Did Mark see the answer that would free him from his guilt as it straggled en masse to the big yellow school bus?

"How old would you say those little kids over there are?" she asked, casually pointing to the youngest children.

Mark shrugged, so deeply troubled that she wasn't sure he saw the children, let alone the conclusion she wanted him to draw from them.

"I don't know. Five? Six?" Silence.

Then she saw the revelation dawn in his bright, green eyes.

"Oh. I was that age, wasn't I."

"Looks like. A little young to see the complexity of adult relationships, huh? Or to understand the significance of Mommy's secret friend? Now let's go back and see if your dad isn't out front waiting for you. It's past time for you two to talk all this out. You can use my office as neutral territory."

"Can you stay?"

Why did he feel he needed her there? She was beginning to think it wasn't necessary to ask, but she had to. Needed to, maybe, though she couldn't bring herself to analyze why.

"Mark, do you have any reason to be afraid of your father?"

Mark looked at her as if her head had just spun completely around. "Afraid? Of Dad? Ms. Lexington, with all the grief I've given my dad, he's never even yelled at me. Maybe that's one of the reasons I kept pushing him."

"That's what I thought, but I had to ask," Xandra said with a smile. "I care about you, Mark, but it's also my job to make sure you're safe. I'm glad you are." She smiled, more relieved than she cared to question.

Mark leaned on the fence heavily, his gaze unfocused. "For a while when he didn't even yell, I thought he didn't care even though he said he did. But when things were coming back to me last night, I remembered something he told me once.

"I got into a shoving match at a campground with some bigger kids who wouldn't let the little ones play on the swings. Dad broke it up and sent this one bigger kid away. Then he knelt down and told all of us that he stepped in because using your strength against someone smaller the way that kid was makes you smaller than they are." Mark grimaced. "I'm not afraid of him. I'm afraid of seeing his disappointment in me."

"Everything's going to be all right. Nothing will change how your father feels about you. And I'll stay, if you think it would help."

"Stay. Please stay. At least this way if I can't say what I have to, you can maybe tell him for me. I'm so ashamed of what I did, but mostly of how I've acted." He looked back at the children climbing on the bus. "You're sure this is a good idea?"

"Mark, look how little and innocent those kindergartners are. Come on. You can do this. Your father deserves the truth. It's past time to talk it all out with him. Believe me, you're hurting him more with silence than with the truth."

Mark scrubbed the remnants of his tears off his cheek. "You really think he can forgive me for being such a brat?"

Xandra nodded. "I'll find your dad and bring him up to the office. You go on ahead. We'll meet you there." She patted him on the shoulder. "It'll be okay, Mark. I promise."

Mark didn't look too sure about her promise, but she was. Adam loved his son unconditionally. She hoped Mark appreciated how wonderful it was to be loved that way by someone. Until she'd found the Lord, she hadn't known, so she could appreciate how truly amazing a feeling it was.

Xandra walked along the line of cars looking for Adam, unsure what kind of car he drove. She scanned all the high-end foreign vehicles, but all had women behind the wheel. Then she noticed a late-model, navy-blue SUV parked at the front of the line. She smiled when she saw a very male arm hanging out of the window. With a jolt she realized she understood his no-nonsense personality pretty well. He might spend millions saving the family home and his old neighbors from developers, but he'd never get rid of a perfectly good car just because it had a few miles on it.

She walked up to the big vehicle, watching in the mirror as Adam slept, unaware of her approach. Then his eyes popped open as if he'd felt her nearing presence. When he focused on her, she felt her stomach take a dip. He had the most lively green eyes. It wasn't the surprising color but the vibrant personality behind them she found arresting. And that worried her far more than did the coming meeting between him and his son.

Chapter Twelve

"**P**lease don't tell me Mark's in trouble again," Adam said, staring at Alexandra's reflection in the mirror. She always looked so cool. So professional at work, even with her hair down as it was today. So different from the woman who'd cuddled her new quarter horse as she helped introduce Dauntless to his new stall.

She shook her head in answer to his question but then added, "More troubled than in trouble. You should be very proud of him, Adam. Rather than act out, he came to see me. He's very upset."

Adam twisted in the seat to face her, no longer content to read her expressions in the mirror. "What's going on?" He'd had a bad feeling about Mark since dinner last night. "He's been acting sort of off since right after my stuff arrived yesterday. More off than usual, I guess I should say. He asked if he could look through a box he'd carried up to my room. It seemed like an okay thing to let him see. It was my office stuff. Just a bunch of commendations and certificates I used to have hanging on the wall to use up some of the space. I thought he might be upset because he saw a wedding photo of me and Mallory in the box.''

Alexandra opened her mouth as if to speak, but closed it and shook her head. ''He'll tell you, I'm sure. He's waiting in my office. He's pretty upset, as I said, so I promised to stay with you two while you talk. I hope that's okay.''

''Anything that helps Mark is okay with me. *Anything*.''

Alexandra led the way to her office, and Adam found himself praying for wisdom. As he'd told her, he wasn't a complete heathen. What was the old saying about there being no atheists in foxholes? Well, he'd been in plenty of foxholes—or reasonable facsimiles, anyway. Maybe more than any man's share of tight spots.

It was just this whole *Christian* thing he couldn't wrap his mind around. He'd always thought of himself as a Christian, but to so many of the people he'd encountered since coming back to the area, it meant more than it ever had to him. He admitted he was curious about how they saw life and how they led theirs with such obvious emotional success.

Alexandra stopped at the end of the hall that led to her office and turned to him. Looking down at her reminded him of his own size, and as always, reminded him of the duty he carried never to use his strength or size to intimidate anyone who wasn't a threat. And he no longer saw Alexandra Lexington as a threat.

"Remember we talked about forgiveness?" she asked. "And about how anger toward your ex-wife might be something you need to be extra-vigilant about hiding from Mark if you couldn't forgive her outright?"

He winced. "I remember." He hadn't gotten very far with the forgiveness part of her advice. "I don't think he knows how I feel. Why do you mention it now?"

"Because your effort is about to get a lot harder. I just thought I should warn you."

"Why is it about to get harder?" He genuinely wanted to know, sick dread having dropped another weight onto his shoulders.

Alexandra shook her head. "I've really said too much already. But I can tell you this. Right now Mark needs you more than he ever has in his entire life. And he's waiting." She gestured toward her office.

As they approached her door, he prayed harder that he would be able to heed her advice on forgiveness, and he reminded himself how seeing the anger he harbored for Mallory could affect Mark.

They found Mark sitting in the dark on the love seat across from Alexandra's desk. He had his back against one of the arms, so he was upright, but with his arms wrapped around his bent knees. He might as well have been curled in a fetal position. Alexandra clicked on the end table lamp, and Mark looked up at them.

"Mark? What's up, buddy?" Adam said as he stepped around Alexandra. He went down on one knee next to Mark, wanting to be as close to his hurting son as he could get.

Mark looked up, dry eyed now, but the evidence that his son had been crying tore at Adam's heart.

"I put it all together," he answered, his voice raw with tears he'd obviously already shed.

Confused, Adam asked, "Put what together?"

"All the lies. I remembered the report card ceremonies. I hated my wallpaper the second time. I scribbled all over it after Jerry put it up. Last night I found your Purple Heart letter, but first I found the letter she wrote you. It was in your wedding picture frame."

Adam felt terrible. He'd put the letter there years ago to remind himself of what Mallory had done to him. He'd never meant for Mark to see it. "I forgot I tucked it in there," Adam said, and swore silently, filled with so many conflicting emotions that his heart felt as if it were a rubber ball bouncing endlessly from one place to another. He felt joy that his son really had missed him, but a soul-deep sorrow and guilt that Mark had been so desperately unhappy and Adam hadn't even known.

He'd told himself the boy was fine in New Mexico. Better off without him. *Good Lord, how could I have been so wrong?*

"Why don't you tell me what happened last night?"

"When I dropped the box, the frame must have broken. The letter fell out and I read it because I recognized Mom's writing. Right after that, you came in and I noticed your leg. That's when it started coming together, like a door in my head opened or something. I had to find the stuff on your Purple Heart, so I asked if I could look through your commendations.''

Adam nodded. He wished he could see where all this was headed. Trying to follow Mark's twisting thought processes was sometimes like tracking the enemy through the densest of jungles.

''What's my Purple Heart got to do with this, son? You've seen my leg before. It's been healed for years. I'm fine.''

Mark's lips pulled into an angry line. ''But you weren't fine when you came back and you were alone. You were alone because we left. You didn't leave *us*.''

Adam flinched, feeling as if Mark had hit him square between the eyes. ''All this time you thought *I* left? But, Mark, I said goodbye to you when I left on that training exercise. I told you I'd be back. Sure, it took longer than I thought, because we were deployed straight from the exercise, but your mother knew. Command called her.''

Mark's eyes rounded with desperation. ''Don't you get it? You're so good you don't get it! She lied to me. But she'd been lying to you for a while by then. And I…I helped,'' he said weakly, as if trying the words out for a reaction. ''I helped!'' he repeated, guilt so thick in his voice it was a wonder he hadn't choked on it. Mark ducked his head then, as if too ashamed to look him in the eye any longer.

Poor kid. He really thought Adam hadn't figured this part out long ago. Of course Mark had known Jerry before they'd left for New Mexico. He'd never understand how a woman who was as protective a mother as Mallory could have done that to her son. It was only one of the reasons for his anger at the woman who'd been the love of his life.

Adam took a deep breath. He was the adult here. He would manage somehow to comfort Mark while hiding his own pain. He would keep his tone neutral, even though the muscles in his back and stomach were bunched into angry knots. "Because you'd met Jerry when I was still around and you didn't tell me? Didn't mention him to me?"

Mark's head snapped up and he looked at Alexandra. She made a hands-off gesture. "I didn't say a word, Mark."

"Son, I had friends in the neighborhood. They'd seen Jerry Beecham hanging around for months, but they didn't think it was their place to say anything to me. They told me about it when I got out of the hospital. I've always known that if she left me for Jerry, he had to have been around for a while when I wasn't there. Mainly because your mother never would have taken you away with him if you didn't know him and weren't comfortable with him. Your mother loved you."

Mark's face started to crumple. "You must hate me. Why would you even want to look at me?"

The pain in his son's eyes was nearly Adam's undoing. *Mallory, what did you do to our child?* "I don't hate you. I love you. You're my son. You were a little boy caught between two people who couldn't make each other happy.''

The pain in Mark's eyes morphed into anger again. ''But she *did* make you happy. Didn't she? Aunt Sky told me last night. She told me how upset you were when you called from the hospital looking for us after you got Mom's letter.''

Adam sighed and raked a hand through his hair. ''Your aunt Skyler has a big mouth,'' he growled.

''She said she was mad at Mom for years for what she did to you.'' Mark studied his face. ''Why didn't you see me more? Was it because I helped, or because Mom hated our visits? Aunt Sky said she thought you were still trying to make Mom happy by not making waves.''

Adam knew it was time to be even more careful. Weighing his words, he hesitated to respond. He opted for the difficult truth, one he'd only just faced after a long talk with his sister, Beth. ''I didn't see you as often as I should have, and that's because I'm a coward, Mark. I didn't want to listen to what a lousy father I was. I was half afraid she was right, but I still couldn't give you up by letting Jerry adopt you. You're my son. It also hurt every time I had to threaten her with court action in order to see you. I love you and I wanted to see you more often. I did whenever I could. And, yeah, it hurt for a long time seeing her with Jerry, but not as much as it hurt losing you to him a little more each year.''

Mark was close to tears now, but there were times

when only the truth would do. Contrary to Alexandra's advice, he thought Mark needed to know how he felt. "Then when I went to pick you up at Skyler's in February, and you looked at me as if I were a stranger, I realized what a big mistake I'd made. Until that moment, I'd thought we had managed to build a pretty good relationship in spite of the long separations. I was devastated, kiddo."

"I needed you after they died, but you didn't call or write," his son charged.

It looked as if Mallory had continued to lie to Mark right up until her death. "Your mother never told you I was deployed all last year, did she."

Mark blinked back his tears again and shook his head. "I guessed you were gone a lot because of the War on Terrorism thing, but I wasn't sure. I tried to tell myself you couldn't help it."

"I told you that day at Sky's house. It was six weeks before I got the letter from her. And after that, you don't just leave in the middle of a war, especially since Sky said you were okay with her. I would have given my right arm to be with you, but there was nothing I could do."

Mark looked down again, shamefaced. "I guess I didn't believe you. I thought you had to give up the SEALs and you put it off as long as you could, or something."

"Mark, I've told you—"

"I know," Mark burst out, "but I've just been so mad at everything. Stuff was all confused in my head when I tried to think. Memories of back then just didn't add up. I didn't know what was true and what was a lie. So it all felt like lies. And the good stuff I remembered, like the report card ceremonies, felt like stupid kid dreams. Then last night, I realized you'd never lied to me. Mom had. And Jerry had. The trouble is, now I can't tell either one of them how I feel. They're gone and I'm left with this *feeling* that I don't know what to do with.''

Adam glanced up at Alexandra and sighed. Now he really got it. He felt the way Mark did, but his son hadn't learned to hide it and control what others saw. This was everything he'd been feeling. It was spilling out of his son all over the place where Adam couldn't ignore it or pretend it didn't matter. He dragged his gaze from the compassion in Alexandra's eyes and turned his attention back to Mark.

"That feeling is anger and hurt, son. I talked to Ms. Lexington about this on Wednesday. She gave me some advice. At the time I didn't fully understand what she was saying, but seeing you now, I guess I get it. She told me I had to forgive your mother because, you see, I've been pretty mad at her myself. Ms. Lexington told me anger takes too much energy, and I've got to tell you, son, I'm tired to the bone right now. So—'' he huffed out a breath ''—I'm going to forgive her for keeping us apart, for leaving me, for lying to you and hurting you with those lies and for the ones she made you tell. The way my anger makes me feel just isn't worth it. You and the new life I'm trying to build for us deserve all my energy. How about you? Aren't you pretty tired, too?''

Mark nodded. "Yeah, and I just figured all this out last night. Man, you must be out on your feet."

Adam chuckled and stood. He *was* tired. Emotionally. But physically he was charged. Like he'd gone into battle and emerged victorious.

"Hey, suppose you go get your books and jacket from your locker and we'll drag our sorry selves home. Or better yet, how about we go over to Laurel Glen and bribe your uncle into letting us borrow a couple of mounts? There are parts of Boyerton you have to see from horseback to appreciate."

Mark nodded, but as he passed Alexandra on his way to the door, he muttered, "Hopefully they're a little less grotesque than the house."

Alexandra snickered as Adam turned toward her. She raised her eyebrow, her expression expectant.

"What?" he asked.

"I'm waiting for you to defend your house. You must like it or you wouldn't have gone to so much trouble to buy it. All I can say is, at least Mark has better taste in architecture than his father."

"You don't like my house?" he asked, pretending to be offended.

She wasn't fooled. "According to Mark, *you* don't like your house."

Caught. Adam grinned helplessly, though he was embarrassed to be so transparent. All in all, ignoring the whole subject of his home seemed like the best course of action. "So, are you game for a ride with us? You must need to unwind as much as Mark and

I do. I can't think you expected this when you came to work this morning.''

She sighed. ''You'd be surprised at the problems that have unexpectedly walked through my door in the last year. This isn't the same world we grew up in, Adam. Even here, in this peaceful-looking community, some of the stories I hear are enough to curl even this,'' she told him, flipping her shining, poker-straight hair carelessly behind her shoulder.

His fingers itched to trail through those silken tresses, and the need he felt jolted him. Wait a minute. *Friendship* was the key word here. And that had nothing to do with where his mind had just strayed. Nothing at all.

Chapter Thirteen

Three hours later Xandra dismounted near Stable Two, giving Dauntless a loving pat. Somewhere along the dark deer track through the woods on the way back from Boyerton, apprehension had burrowed itself into her heart. And so she'd begun analyzing the situation and facing the truth. The ride had been a mistake. A huge mistake. She'd had no business going along at all. She was Mark's counselor and nothing more. And father and son no longer needed her.

And she certainly didn't need them.

She looked back at the practice ring where they were talking to Beth and Jack and C.J. and Cole Taggert. Adam stood out from the other two men in a way she couldn't quite grasp. It wasn't his height, since Jack was the tallest of the men in the group. It wasn't his lighter hair, though it did glint with a golden light in the bright sunshine. Perhaps it was his military bearing, the authority he exuded even when relaxed.

Whatever it was, she told herself, it didn't matter. It couldn't matter. He was filtering into her thoughts too often, and that had to be a bad sign. She couldn't let this opportunity to escape pass her by. She had to put Dauntless away and get out of there.

Georgie, a grizzled man in his late sixties, ambled out of the stable at the moment of her decision. She knew he'd worked at Laurel Glen when Ross Taggert, the current owner, was only Mark's age. And she knew Georgie dreaded retirement. Jack gave him all the easiest chores to keep him feeling useful; putting Dauntless away and rubbing him down was right up his alley.

Xandra sent the old man a happy, if false, smile. "Georgie, how are you today?" she asked, genuinely interested in spite of her hurry—okay, near panic— and needful of his help.

"Miss Xandra," he said, tipping his baseball cap. "I'm fine. Just fine. Beautiful day, isn't it?"

"Fantastic. I wonder if you have the time to do me a huge favor? I just remembered something I'd forgotten I have to do, and I don't have time to take care of Dauntless."

Georgie smiled, his much-lined face wreathed in joy. "Well, sure thing, miss. It's no trouble at all. I was just going to ask Jack what he needs me to do next. You saved me the walk."

"You're terrific," she told Georgie, then checked the group across the yard. They were still talking and laughing, not looking her way. "Next time I come by, I'll bring you some of my chocolate-chip cookies. Beth says they're your favorite kind."

"Sure are. But that isn't necessary. Working with Dauntless is a pure pleasure."

"You have no idea how important this is. Thanks so much," she told the old handler. She turned Dauntless's reins over and gave the horse's neck another quick pat, then took off toward the door to Stable Three, her plan of escape fully formed.

She knew the rear door of that stable opened from the inside onto the parking lot where she'd left her car. This way she bypassed the small knot of people gathered in the yard next to the neighboring stable. With a sigh of relief, she stepped out into the sunlight again only yards from her car.

If she could just get away from Laurel Glen today, she reasoned, there was no need to see Adam again. He and Mark were on the right track, and guidance counselors only saw the parents of their troubled students. Sure, Beth was her friend, but it really looked as if she and Jack might decide to give living in Colorado at the Circle A a try. She could visit Beth there. And, as much as she hated to do it, if seeing Adam at Laurel Glen grew too uncomfortable, she could move Dauntless to another facility.

Relief flooded her as she opened her car door, but a split second later she froze at the sound of her name.

"Yes?" she asked turning around, trying not to look like a kid with a cookie jar in hand.

"Where are you off to in such a hurry?" asked Adam.

"Home. There are several reports waiting on my desk that I have to get ready for tomorrow." It wasn't a lie, except that she was only an hour from completing them.

"I was hoping to take you to dinner. I wanted to thank you for all you did for us."

Dinner? She swallowed. She liked Adam…more than she should. More than she could handle. "No thanks are necessary, really. And dinner certainly isn't—I was doing my job. Besides that, Beth is my friend. I wanted to help her nephew. Why don't you take Mark to dinner and celebrate your breakthrough?"

"Jack asked him if he wanted to work with C.J. learning English tack and maybe get his feet wet with a little jumping. So you see, I've been deserted," he said, trying to look pathetic and missing by a mile. He was just too devastatingly handsome for his own good. And hers. She had to get out of there!

"I really can't take the time."

"You have to eat sometime."

"And I will, at my desk. I'm sorry, Adam, I rearranged my schedule today as much as I can afford to. Tell Mark goodbye and good luck with the lessons. Okay?"

"Sure. I guess I'll see you around Laurel Glen or town." He backed away. "Thanks again."

Xandra watched Adam disappear around the corner of Stable Four. He looked so alone suddenly. What made her think his being handsome meant he had a full social calendar? He'd been gone a long time and knew very few people in town. She felt small and mean as she stood noticing that his broad shoulders look bowed, as if something—maybe time—weighed on them. They had sagged when she'd finally gotten her point across, she realized now, but she steeled herself against any pangs of conscience.

He is only the father of a student, she told herself sternly. *The brother of a friend,* she added for good measure. *And that is all he'll ever be. Ever could be.*

So why did she feel so awful?

Xandra almost called him back, but instead forced herself to get in her car and drive home, telling herself she hadn't just made a huge mistake. It wasn't easy to do with an ache in her chest and the hollow feeling of loss in the pit of her stomach.

Why do I feel this way, Lord? she asked, but even she knew she was refusing to listen for an answer. Sometimes she was such a coward it shocked even her.

Mark watched Ms. Lexington's car as she drove down the drive headed toward Indian Creek Road. He sighed in relief. He didn't like the way his father looked at her. Or the way she sometimes looked at him. And he didn't know for sure why his dad had run off the way he had to catch her. Or even why he had asked her to go for the ride with them, for that matter. But Mark had an idea.

He was nearly sure Adam wanted to date her. And that was just so wrong!

Ms. Lexington was *his* friend. Mark did not want her dating his father. That would lead only to disaster. And Mark would lose her. Over the years he'd met and really liked more of his father's girlfriends than he could count. Every time his father had flown him to California, which had been once or twice a year, he'd introduced Mark to yet another really nice lady. But then when Mark would ask about her the next time they saw each other, his father would make one excuse or another why the nice woman was no longer around.

Now that Aunt Sky had explained about his father still loving Mark's mother all that time, it made sense. And the anger his father had confessed toward his mother proved Mark was right. That Aunt Sky was right. You didn't get that mad at someone unless they could still hurt you. Unless you still loved the person.

Every time his dad took him to see Aunt Sky and his grandparents on those California visits, Mark would watch how great his dad and Sky got along. She was so much like Mark's mother that it made sense now. He was sure Adam would be happy with Sky if he'd just give it a chance. That would be so awesome. They'd be the family Mark had always wanted them to be.

And Ms. Lexington would stay safely his.

Adam saw Alexandra go into the café as he stepped out of the post office onto the high wooden sidewalk of the little town center. He hadn't seen her in a week, and he was pretty disconcerted to find he'd missed her as much as he had. Maybe not *her,* but the friendship they'd begun to build, he ventured.

He was lonely and that was apt to get worse now that Beth and Jack had decided to move to Colorado. Adam's relationship with Mark was much better, but the kid had his own life and Adam refused to smother him with too much attention.

Sully was company, but their memories were so tied up in killing and death that he wasn't comfortable sharing old war stories in Mark's presence. Besides, Adam didn't want the rest of his life to revolve around the past. He had to build a future away from the SEAL teams and the Navy. But he also couldn't be only a parent, either.

With that in mind, he followed Alexandra into the café. She was sitting alone, so he walked up to the table. ''Alexandra, how have you been?'' he asked, standing next to her.

Her eyes were wide with surprise when her head snapped up. ''Oh! Uh…Adam. How are you?'' Gripped in her hands, she held a paper napkin. She tore it in half. ''Uh, I mean…how are you and Mark getting along?'' She swallowed, her hands fluttered the ragged halves of the napkin, and her eyes darted around the room.

It was as if she were checking to see who was there to watch them talking. Adam frowned. ''Is something wrong?''

"Of course not. I'm just waiting for someone. I'm sorry, Adam, but I can't invite you to join us."

Thinking it might be work related, he nodded, perfectly willing to accept her explanation. "Oh, that's okay. I just wondered if you were free tonight. We never got to have that thank-you dinner."

Alexandra stared up at him, her blue-gray eyes wide...dismayed. Then one of her seemingly out-of-control hands knocked over her water glass. She swung her legs out of the booth and jumped up to avoid the spreading cascade. As she did she stepped back and bumped into him.

Reflex action had Adam reaching for her upper arms to steady her. He was surprised to find tremors buffeting her body. "Are you sure there's nothing wrong?" he asked her, his mouth only inches from her ear.

Before she could answer, a strident voice behind him snapped, "Get your hands off my daughter. I've heard what that son of yours said about my Jason."

He turned and saw Mrs. Lexington standing there. He wondered how eyes the soft color of Alexandra's could look so hard. This meeting promised to be as annoying and convoluted as the last.

"You warn him not to repeat any more lies," she went on. "He's listening to the ravings of an unbalanced woman, just as I'm sure you are. You didn't know my son. He was a good boy."

Who did she mean was "unbalanced"? Beth or Alexandra? He'd talk to Mark about repeating private things, but he knew Beth hadn't spoken of her past with Mark. So was she talking about her own daughter? He found he didn't care which woman she meant.

"Lady, if there's anybody unbalanced in this town, it's you, and from what I hear, your son was a monster, not a good boy."

He turned to Alexandra, expecting to see anger at her mother—but he saw embarrassment. At him? At her mother? Or because her mother suspected they were friends? Her reason for turning down dinner seemed flimsier than ever.

"Would I be right in guessing you'd like me to leave?"

Her gaze cut to her mother, then to the floor. "Just go. Okay?"

Adam turned on his heel. It looked as if he'd misread her once again. Helping him and Mark had clearly been only a job and a way to pay Beth back for Mitzy Lexington's tongue. But now it was clear that she was still influenced by her family, still dancing to her mother's tune in public.

Alexandra wasn't the first woman he'd misinterpreted. As he climbed behind the wheel of his SUV, Adam tried to console himself with the fact that at least this time the woman wasn't his wife.

"Alexandra Balfour, how could you? You have a husband who loves and adores you."

Lord give me strength and calm, Xandra prayed as she wiped off the seat of the booth and sat down across from her mother. This was what she'd worried about from the second she'd looked up and seen

Adam standing there. If her mother told Michael she'd seen Xandra with another man, it could set him off again. And she just wasn't ready for a direct confrontation with him yet. If ever.

"Don't just sit there staring. I'd like an explanation," her mother demanded, smiling falsely—a smile never reached her eyes. It was, of course, her way of hiding the confrontational nature of the encounter from prying eyes. Dressed impeccably at all times, she ran her numerous charities with the same precision as she did her wardrobe. But, sad to say, Xandra didn't think she had a charitable bone in her fashionably thin body.

"I don't have a husband anymore, Mother," Xandra said quietly as her mother opened her purse.

Her mother's piercing blue eyes snapped up and bore into hers. It was all Xandra could do not to flinch. "In the eyes of God—" her mother said, her lips straight and as hard as her eyes.

Something inside Xandra lurched. She wouldn't listen to a woman who thought she could pay her way into heaven spout off about what she thought God had and had not said. "Don't presume to speak for the Lord. I'm not the one who broke my marriage vows, as you well know but refuse to believe. And, in case you've forgotten, my name is no longer Balfour.

"As far as Adam goes, you are more wrong than you can imagine about what you just saw. I bumped into the man after spilling my water all over. He is the father of a student who stopped to say hello. And for his trouble you embarrassed him."

Her mother grabbed her hand. "You need help, Alexandra. You should see Lionel Avery. He'd be able to help you."

"The way he did last time?" When she'd come home with Michael last year for a charity ball her parents had invited them to attend, her mother had seen her nervousness and had called her old friend to the house. Ashamed, Xandra hadn't been able to bring herself to tell her mother why she was so nervous, but she had told Dr. Avery. He'd given her medication to calm her nerves, and she'd taken it, hoping it would help her cope with her anxiety enough so she could regain some of her fighting spirit. But she hadn't needed medication. She'd needed freedom and safety.

Instead of helping her get free, the medication had put her in a fog during the stay in Pennsylvania. What was worse, Dr. Avery told her mother some of what she'd said about Michael, thinking to help. But her mother had heard "anxiety medication" and the abuse charges and believed Xandra was unbalanced. Then her mother had gone to Michael, begging him to get her poor daughter the help she needed.

When they'd arrived home, Michael's rage had been unequaled. That was the first time she'd feared for her life and the first time clothing hadn't hidden her bruises. It had also been the last.

"Lionel Avery tried. I tried," her mother was saying. "It's you who refused his help and mine."

"No, Mother. You and Dr. Avery made it all worse. I didn't need pills. I needed rescuing."

And rescue had come in the guise of a stranger's help. Pedro Santiago, the son of Michael's new housekeeper, had stepped in after his mother reported what she'd heard the night before. The next morning, after Michael had left for a meeting, Pedro had come to the back door and told her about the domestic violence program in San Diego. He had with him a bus ticket and a disguise. Then 'he'd hidden her under a blanket in his old rattletrap of a car and driven her to the next town and the bus.

Xandra had left the pills behind, but not the fear or the shame. She should have rescued herself.

"What did you want when you asked me to meet you here?" she demanded, tired of dealing with her mother. It was exhausting trying to communicate with people who refused to look at events and truth in a logical way.

"Someone saw you riding at Laurel Glen with that man," Mitzy Lexington charged in a hissing whisper. "I wanted to know if my daughter had betrayed not only her husband but her family."

"My husband was a sadistic monster just like my brother. Just recently he sent me a copy of our wedding album on what would have been our anniversary."

"Really, Alexandra, that was just a sweet gesture. He told me he was going to do it."

"The first page said 'till death do us part.'"

"You see. He hasn't been able to forget you. He hasn't given up hope even after all you've done to him."

"All I've…" Xandra stood. Worry, fear and anger threatened to overwhelm her. Nothing she could say would stop Mitzy Lexington from doing her worst and passing on what she saw as important information. "As I said, Adam is the son of a student. Mark was with us. I was there to help them talk to each other. You have a blind spot where Michael is concerned, Mother. A dangerous one. And if you call Michael and tell him these things, it may well get me killed!"

Chapter Fourteen

Xandra barely heard Pastor Dillon's sermon that next Sunday morning. It had been two days since her run-in with her mother, and she'd yet to find any peace or stop looking over her shoulder. She knew she had to apologize to Adam for the way her mother had treated him, and if she saw him she would, but she had more than that to deal with right now.

Since coming to the Lord, Xandra had struggled with the reality of her parents. How could she honor two people who had done nothing over the years but earn her contempt? And how could she witness to people she had been all but invisible to all her life? She wasn't feeling sorry for herself or looking for sympathy when she admitted that her place in the family had always been as the one to receive criticism, the one who didn't measure up.

To her mother, Jason, her firstborn, had been everything. He could do no wrong. Mitzy Lexington had coddled and spoiled him. Just like food that had spoiled, Jason had been good for no one, especially himself.

And then there was her father. He'd always been so preoccupied with business that over the years he'd become nothing but a rubber stamp of her mother's decisions in personal matters. She could hear him still. *"Take it to your mother. She's the wife. I'm just here to support her decisions,"* he would say, rather than listen to whatever problem Xandra had. Geoffrey Lexington was a money machine, not a father.

She thought of Adam and his effort to be the best father he could be for Mark. She wondered if he would treat a woman he loved with that same remarkable dedication. His invitation to dinner returned to haunt her once again, as did her mother's reaction to seeing their accidental meeting.

Most of all, it was the remark her mother had made about Xandra still being married to Michael in the eyes of God. *Would* the loving, just God she had come to know expect her to risk her life to remain married to an abuser? Or was divorce okay only as long as she remained alone?

Alone.

"Alone" had never seemed like anything other than freedom until very recently. But these days, everywhere she looked the world had paired off. And then there were the children. It seemed as if babies and pregnant women were coming out of the woodwork around the Tabernacle and in the teachers' lounge at Indian Creek High. Though she was sincerely glad she'd bought Dauntless for all the joy he was bringing into her life, she was afraid the void she'd hoped he would fill was still there.

She had wanted babies. Still did. Michael hadn't wanted to share her at first, and, foolishly, rather than seeing that as odd, she'd been flattered. Then she'd become determined not to bring a child into the nightmare her world had become. The nightmare had lasted a little less than two years, but now Xandra wondered if it hadn't ruined the rest of her life.

Again she thought of Adam and his dinner invitation. She was so out of touch with her emotions, her desires, she hadn't understood what she was feeling. She'd finally figured out why that invitation had rattled her so badly—because she'd been tempted to accept.

Beth had told her over and over for the past year that she had to learn to trust her judgment again. Until meeting Adam, Xandra hadn't thought it would ever matter. And now she had to face the truth. It did. It mattered a lot. Plus her mother had added a new worry. Was she morally tied to Michael for the rest of her life?

"Now *that* is the face of someone I've really bummed out," she heard Jim Dillon say from the pew just in front of her.

Xandra focused her eyes on her smiling pastor as he sank sideways into the pew, hooking an arm over the back. She looked around. Everyone but a few stragglers off to the left were gone. She had really zoned out.

"Life has bummed me out, Pastor Jim. You had nothing to do with it. I confess I heard almost nothing of what you said. I promise to get the tape," she said, forcing herself to grin. Then she sighed and let the false smile fade. It was bad enough to lie to herself, but to her pastor?

"Got a minute?" she asked.

"All the time you like." He chuckled. "Holly's on another campaign to teach me to cook. With a new baby on the way, she's worried the twins will starve if Ian's away at camp when the baby arrives."

"Another baby," she sighed, unthinking.

The pastor's eyebrow arched. "That was one wistful sigh. You have anyone in mind for a father?"

Xandra swallowed. She guessed she was pretty transparent. "Am I allowed to?"

"I know you came to the Lord last year, since you answered an altar call here. What were the circumstances of your divorce?"

It's better for him to know than to wonder, she told herself. After taking a deep breath, she said, "Michael was unfaithful and physically and mentally abusive. I literally ran for my life. Beth took me in at New Life Inn when I got back here."

Jim Dillon nodded. "You didn't go to your parents for help?"

"They've sided with Michael. In their defense, he's very charming while appearing to be unassuming and not a bit threatening. He certainly fooled me. But still…"

"Still, I'd think they would have reached out to help you."

"We've never been close. But I don't want to scandalize them with my behavior. My parents are the pillars of their church but they don't know the Lord. They're relying on donations to buy their way into heaven. Anyway, the other day my mother said I'm still married to Michael in the eyes of God. I told her she was wrong, but now I wonder if I didn't speak from my own hopes and desires and not from Scripture."

Pastor Jim sighed. "Divorce is one of the great controversies in the Church. I've had people come to me and ask, 'If God can forgive murder, why can't He forgive me for marrying the wrong man or woman?' There is no simple answer. Each circumstance is different.

"In Matthew chapter five, Jesus said that sexual immorality was a reason for divorce. Adultery didn't play a part in my divorce from Holly, and neither of us felt free to marry afterward." He smiled. "Except to remarry each other, which the Lord managed to bring about.

"A believer has two choices in the case of adultery by his or her partner: forgive the affair and stay, or leave."

Jim Dillon pursed his lips, thinking for a moment. "In your case, because of the abuse, I could never advise you to return to your abuser. I'd also say that because there was adultery, you should be free to marry again if you want that. All that said, you weren't a believer when any of that happened. What that means, in my interpretation and according to several biblical scholars along with Paul, is that you have a new life in Christ, and sins and mistakes of the past no longer bind you. I have to say I think your mother is wrong. *Is* there some lucky guy who prompted all this?''

Xandra shrugged. ''Not exactly. I got a dinner invitation. I like the person but I'm unsure. Michael is a very frightening man. And I'd thought Michael was this mild-mannered person—my brother's opposite. This man who asked me out seems to be all that is patient and kind. But he's also a lot of things they were. Wealthy. Charming. Handsome.''

''And you don't trust your judgment. You're afraid to step out and make the wrong decision.''

''How do I know if I'm right or not? I know all men aren't abusers. I know there are good relationships. I'm honestly not afraid of all men. But I *am* leery of this one. Maybe of any one I'd choose. I can't make the same mistake again. I just can't.''

''But you don't think you have reason to mistrust this man? You don't think this is the Holy Spirit whispering a warning?''

She thought of Adam. She'd seen him angry and it had worried her. But later, when she'd thought about it, he'd been completely in control of his anger. Very different from Michael. Unlike the rest of Michael's behavior, which was almost maniacally controlled, his anger was always completely out of control. Her brother had been the same.

"No. I think it's me. I think I'm afraid to care about a man again. And I don't know what to do about it."

Pastor Dillon shrugged. "I can only tell you that the Lord doesn't give us a spirit of fear. That comes from Satan. I can tell you what I do when something has me all but paralyzed with fear."

"You?"

The pastor looked amused by her astonishment. Jim Dillon was the most together person she'd ever met.

"What, you think I'm immune? Fear strikes all of us, as does temptation. I face every day knowing I'm only a drink away from destroying my life. Only prayer gets me past that. When I find myself afraid to move forward on a project or a sermon or life in general, I stop dithering and pray. I ask the Lord to step in. I trust Him to close doors He doesn't want me to walk through.

"Maybe it's time to finally put your life in God's hands, Alexandra. If you can't make a decision, let Him make it. Trust Him to direct your path with this man who interests you."

"And what about my parents? What about my witness to them?"

"I understand your worry over your witness to your parents. Have you tried talking to them? Witnessing to them directly about what being a Christian has come to mean to you?"

"They say the Tabernacle is a cult. That I've fallen under your evil power."

Pastor Dillon frowned and huffed out a sigh, then

grinned wryly. "There's a reference in Matthew—chapter seven, verse six. 'Do not give what is holy to the dogs; nor cast your pearls before swine, lest they trample them under their feet, and turn and tear you in pieces.' Now, I'm not calling your parents dogs or swine, but they do sound as if they've hardened their hearts. Christ himself told His disciples to give up on people who refused to listen. If your parents are meant to hear His call, they will. But if their hearts are hardened to His Gospel, you can't restrict the life the Lord would have for you because of them. It would be a terrible waste of the life He's given you if you remained stubbornly alone and He has a man for you out there."

Xandra left the Tabernacle a few minutes later with her theological doubts put to rest, leaving only one question unanswered. The one only she could answer.

What to do about Adam?

Should she take any action at all? she wondered as she climbed behind the wheel of her car. After all, he'd only asked her to dinner to thank her for helping him and Mark. The rest of her thoughts about him were her problem.

Pastor Jim said her fear didn't come from the Lord, and she readily accepted that as the truth. Adam had never made a threatening move toward her. Each doubt she'd had about him had come from her, not his actions. She'd thought him controlling because Michael had been. But Adam had dispelled her theory—her fear—with a simple statement explaining that SEALs live a life of teamwork. Then, when she'd questioned Mark about the possibility that Adam might be a physical threat, Mark, after shooting her a look that questioned her sanity, had unequivocally dispelled her concern.

So where did that leave her?

She sighed. First things first. She started the car and put it in gear. She had to apologize to Adam for her mother's behavior at the café.

Chapter Fifteen

Adam looked down from the attic, surprised to see Alexandra's white convertible cruising down the drive toward the house. He watched as she climbed out, pulling a scarf off, her hair loose and tousled. Mark ran out the side door below him and shouted a greeting.

So she was checking up on Mark, her pet project, he thought sourly as the murmur of their voices drifted up to him. Last night Mark had mentioned something that had happened while Alexandra was helping him get his head straight. She'd asked if he were afraid of Adam. Adam had tried not to be insulted, but it wasn't easy after the way she'd treated him. It was best for him to just stay away from her. She'd made it more than plain in that café that she couldn't possibly be here to see him, so he had no problem avoiding her, even if he appeared rude.

Alexandra's laughter drifted up to him, and once

again he made an effort to ignore her. He'd taken Mark to church but hadn't gone in today. He'd told himself he didn't want to be inside on such a beautiful day. But Adam didn't like lying to himself. He'd seen her car and hadn't wanted to run into her again after twice being rebuffed.

He was, quite frankly, embarrassed that he hadn't gotten the message the first time. Call him an arrogant fool, but, in his defense, he wasn't used to having dinner invitations tossed back in his face. Women had always liked him, and he liked them right back. But now he wondered if it had been the uniform all along that had attracted them. He'd certainly been told enough times by Mallory that his being a member of one of the country's most elite fighting units had blinded her to the reality of military life.

"Commander! Lady here to see you!" Sully bellowed up at him out of a first-floor window.

Adam couldn't believe his ears. Him? She was here to see *him?* Curious and intrigued, he hotfooted it down to meet her in the foyer. She stood with her back to the stairs, looking at what was supposed to be the dining room. He managed to slow his footsteps before she realized he was there.

Even in a pair of jeans and a well-worn blazer, Alexandra easily outshone the setting. The dining room framing her was devoid of furnishings and in sad shape. Its golden silk walls were slightly soot stained, its once gleaming floors dulled from years of minimal maintenance, and the wainscoting was chipped and scarred. Sully had cleaned the crystal chandelier that Adam knew was antique Waterford. Unfortunately, rather than resembling something out of a chamber of horrors the way it had when draped in cobwebs and coated with dust, it looked like exactly what it was—a lonely remnant of remembered elegance. Even if it was one of the more expensive appointments in the house, it wasn't his taste. The whole house wasn't his taste.

Unfortunately, Alexandra Lexington, he realized at that moment, was exactly his taste.

She turned to him and grimaced. ''You could always put the chandelier on eBay, I suppose,'' she said. Then her eyes widened in shock.

Adam burst out laughing. She'd insulted his home. His mother's taste. By all rights he should be insulted too. But he couldn't stop laughing.

''I'm so sorry,'' she said loudly over his laughter, trying not to smile and blushing becomingly. ''I hope it isn't your favorite part of the house.''

His laughter had been all but spent, but that set him off again. Finally he controlled himself by remembering what had started his mother on her overblown decorating campaign. ''My father had it shipped here from some castle in England. It was like a trigger for my mother. She redecorated the room to go with it. Then the hall wasn't formal enough, then the parlor. I was pretty small, but I remember the rules of the house changed almost overnight. This place went from being a home to being a museum and my dog got banished to the barn. They took most of those things with them,'' he explained, and gestured to the empty rooms, deciding as he paused that it was time to cut short the small talk. Once again she had pulled information from him with no effort at all. Why did she have to be so easy to talk to?

"So what brings you here?"

She straightened her shoulders. "I came to apologize."

Adam hooked his thumbs in his front belt loops. What was he supposed to say to that? *Oh, don't worry, I'm used to being humiliated by women I find interesting.* "What exactly are you apologizing for?" he asked, deciding the fewer words he spoke, the less likely his ego was to get stomped on again.

"My mother," she replied.

Okay, now he was getting annoyed. "I thought we'd established that if I'm not responsible for my parents, you aren't responsible for yours."

She stared at him, looking a bit uncertain in the face of his building annoyance. "Then why are you mad?" she asked. "And don't tell me you're not. Your eyes are practically shooting sparks."

So much for hiding his feelings. "Fine. I don't like it when someone is embarrassed to be seen with me. I've been treated like a pariah over the years when I was in uniform, but I knew that wasn't really personal. It was what I represented to some people. The other day was personal. Real personal. I'm sorry if my second invitation put you off. If you'd told me I was the last guy in the world you'd share a meal with the first time I asked, you would have spared us both the second embarrassing invitation."

Her jaw dropped. She stared at him, clearly horrified. Then those hypnotic and changeable eyes teared up. She blinked and took a breath. "You thought…I'm so sorry. Oh, Adam. It was my *mother*."

She thought that would make him feel better? "I see. You were just ashamed to have your *mother* see you with me. Thank you, you have no idea how much better that makes me feel!"

"No! You really don't understand. I'm so sorry." She squeezed the bridge of her nose as if fighting a headache and muttered what sounded like "idiots."

Adam took a step back. Away from caring. Away from even wanting to care. What was it about her that disarmed him in all ways? "I can't tell you how little your apology means at this point," he said, hoping to cover his true feelings.

"I'm sure. Please. I wasn't trying to be insulting," she explained, her tone edged with exasperation.

"Well, you succeeded, anyway," he told her. He could see her distress building, and his heart softened toward her again. Something didn't add up. "I think you're going to have to tell me what you're sorry for. I'm obviously clueless."

Now *she* looked annoyed. "Well, of course you are. If you weren't so unnerving, we'd never have had any disagreements."

"So now it's my fault?"

"No! Just shut up, okay? Do you have somewhere we could sit down? This isn't going the way I rehearsed."

She'd rehearsed this? Touched and amused, he smiled. "We have a couple of rooms set up down here where we live like real people. Family room or my office?"

She closed her eyes as if trying to clear her thoughts, then opened them and said, "This is…um… personal. I don't want Mark overhearing."

"Office," he said, gesturing through the parlor. Time had been no more kind to this room. It, too, was devoid of much furniture save a console table and lamp he'd rescued from the attic and stuck between two ten-foot-tall windows so there'd be a light source in there at night.

He guided her to a small secondary hall that led to the rear of the house and several smaller rooms. One of them Adam had set up as his office. It had once been his grandfather's study and the floor-to-ceiling mahogany bookcases that lined the walls were still nearly full of his books. Only the more expensive first editions had gone with his parents.

Twin burgundy leather sofas bracketed a fireplace with an intricately carved sandstone surround and mantel. He nodded toward the sofas and followed her across the room. Once she'd settled, he moved to the other one, choosing to sit at the opposite end. It was less intimate that way, and he didn't want her too close. Something happened to his brain whenever she came near, and he had a feeling he'd better keep a clear head.

"So what's this all about?" he asked as he crossed

his ankle over his knee. He hoped he looked more relaxed than he felt.

"My mother. But not the way you seem to think. I'm divorced, but my mother feels I'm still married to Michael. Among other things, I worried that she'd make another scene in front of you. Her opinion started to worry me, so today I talked to Pastor Jim about my mother, about my divorce."

"Your divorce was a spiritual problem for you?" He'd been divorced. All it had meant to him was that he'd failed, that he was free and didn't want to be. He had thought Alexandra had wanted the divorce.

She looked down at her hands. "What it meant spiritually wasn't something I'd even thought about before this. Pastor Jim says that because Michael was unfaithful, he broke our vows and so my divorcing him was justified. And that since all that happened before I came to Christ, it matters even less."

"So you feel better about what your mother said."

Her gaze rose and collided with his. She nodded slowly. "Yes. Yes, I do."

He studied her. She'd never asked these questions before he'd invited her to dinner? Had his invitation merely gotten her thinking in general, or had she only turned him down for her principles? Her expression gave him no clue what her answer would be if he asked. When she said nothing more, he realized he had no choice but to stick his neck out again.

He broke eye contact, drumming his fingers on the arm of the sofa. "Are you saying you only turned me down because of your mother's opinion on your divorce, or was it because of other reasons you haven't gone into yet?''

"Both," she admitted, then bit her bottom lip before going on. "But I don't think the other things matter anymore. At least I hope not. I'm putting those in the Lord's hands.''

He sat forward, and their eyes locked. "Dinner tonight? Say, around seven?" he asked. Then, since she'd come clean, he added, "And, Alexandra, just so you know, the invitation has nothing to do with Mark.''

She smiled and the day got a lot brighter. "Call me Xandra. And seven's fine. Where shall we meet?''

Xandra stared into the rest-room mirror at seven o'clock that night, wondering what she had done. "You've lost your mind, Xandra," she told her reflection as she tried to freshen her lipstick with a shaking hand. What had she been thinking? How had an apology wound up as a dinner date? And why had she decided Adam Boyer wasn't a threat?

He was a SEAL.

He'd been trained to kill.

In probably a hundred different ways!

The Lord doesn't give us a spirit of fear. That comes from Satan. Pastor Dillon's words of wisdom and counsel burst through the clamor of her panic.

She took a deep breath and closed her eyes. *All right, Lord, I'll give him a chance. It's in Your hands. Just, please, close all doors I shouldn't walk through.*

Tossing her lipstick into her purse, she fussed with

the cowl neck of her pink angora sweater, pushed the sleeves up, then pulled them down a little. Checking the seams of her straight skirt, she turned and caught sight of the door behind her in the mirror. She turned and faced the door, put her hand on the knob, and then, on a deep inhale, twisted it. The door opened smoothly, so, trusting the Lord to guide her, she walked through it.

Standing only a few feet away was Adam. He must have arrived since she'd gone in to freshen up and gain her composure. His golden, honey-colored hair shone under the track lighting overhead as he scanned the lobby and bar for her. He was dressed casually in a navy-blue sweater and tan cotton pants. As if he sensed her presence, Adam turned and smiled.

And she knew. She just knew. It felt almost as if the Lord spoke the words directly into her heart.

She was safe with this man.

Chapter Sixteen

"So, what do you think of Beth's news?" Xandra asked Adam a week after that first momentous date. She looked around as she stepped out of the stable. The sun was setting, casting a golden glow over Laurel House's Pennsylvania fieldstone facade. The grass was now a cheery green and the trees and bushes had begun to thicken and green up with tender little leaves or pretty pink or white flowers, the way they always did in mid-April.

"I think she'll be a great mother," Adam said with a quick smile. Glancing over at Xandra he added, "I'm going to miss her."

"You can visit her in Colorado," she said, and leaned back against the practice ring fence. A lonely shadow seemed to dim his bright eyes. It wasn't the first time she'd seen it. "Are you sorry you moved back here only to have her move away?"

He looked over her head for a moment, taking in

the scenery. Then his gaze lowered to hers. "I have Mark. That's more than I've had for a long time. What about you?" he asked as he braced his arm on the fence above her head.

Having him standing so close made her pulse go haywire. "What—" she swallowed "—about me?"

He moved closer, his eyes slightly hooded, his breath warm on her cheek. "Do I have—?"

She'd never know if he meant to end with "you," because his lips touched hers, and the word he breathed was muffled. The world spun away in the space of a heartbeat. The feel of Adam's arm wrapping around her waist and the hard wall of his chest under her hands became her world. Lost in the wonder of his kiss, of having him hold her so gently and firmly at the same time, she wasn't prepared for the sudden end. Suddenly Adam moaned and backed away, letting go of her as if she were electrified.

"I—" He took a shaky breath, misery invading his eyes. "I should go. I'm sorry. I have to find Mark. I have to leave."

"Adam, what—"

"No. I can't— I have to go. We'll talk. Later." He held out one hand in a gesture that said he was helpless to explain what was wrong. "Later," he said again. "Right now, I really have to go."

And he did. Had he not been so deliberate about the gait that carried him toward the golden sunset, she would have said he ran. Ran away? Adam? What had just happened?

Xandra stood staring after him until a scuffing

sound drew her attention. She whirled toward it. Mark approached from the shadow of the adjoining barn.

"Your father went to find you."

"I know. I, uh, I sort of hung back so I could warn you. My dad's great, but he isn't a good bet, Ms. Lexington."

"Not a good bet?"

Mark shook his head. "You wouldn't believe how many nice ladies have tried with him. It's my aunt Sky, you see. You should see them together. He loves her but he won't admit it. She looks just like Mom, see, so he won't get involved with her. You can't trust the things he says and does sometimes. I just don't want you to get…you know, hurt."

Xandra regarded Mark. What was he up to? Adam had talked about Skyler James, Mark's aunt, and he'd never indicated more than an in-law relationship with his ex-wife's sister. But he had talked about Mallory Beecham and the helpless love he'd continued to feel long after her betrayal. Maybe Mark was right and Adam was a hopeless case, but Skyler as the reason just didn't ring true.

"Do you object to my seeing your father socially?"

Mark shrugged. "Like I said, I just don't want you getting your heart broken. You're my friend, too, so I figured I had a right to protect you."

She tried to smile reassuringly but wasn't sure she'd pulled it off. Adam, not Mark, had her very confused. "Thank you, but you don't have to worry. I won't get hurt. I've put my trust in God, Mark. I promise, He'll protect my heart. I think you'd better go find your father. He seemed to be in a hurry to leave.''

A week had passed, and as Xandra sat in her office filling in her regular Monday report, she paused, wondering if Adam had any concept of time. Did he know what "later" meant to most people?

She'd put her trust in God and that was the only thing that kept her from calling Adam. It wasn't that she didn't understand that their kiss had been something out of the ordinary. Or that he'd been hurt and treated abysmally by his former wife. But she missed him!

As if she'd willed it, Xandra's phone rang from an outside line. The number displayed in the caller ID window set her heart pounding. It was Adam. *Calm down,* she ordered herself silently. *He could be calling about Mark.* After a week of silence and Adam's unmistakable evasion of her, she was more than a little reluctant to get her hopes up.

"Xandra, it's Adam. Please don't hang up," he hurried to say before she could even greet him. His voice was tinged with desperation.

"Now, why would I hang up on a friend?" she asked in as noncommittal a tone as she could manage. She was thankful he wasn't there, though, or her grin would give her away.

He exhaled. "Because this particular friend has less sense than God gave a guppy."

She snickered but managed to cover the phone in

time. He sounded absolutely miserable. "A guppy. How the mighty have fallen. So you're afraid you've given SEALs everywhere a bad name, huh?"

He didn't laugh at her joke. "No. I'm afraid I hurt you. And I miss you. Have lunch with me and I'll try to explain."

Xandra glanced at the clock. "All right. How about Leo's Deli on Walnut Lane?"

A long silence ensued. "Terrific," he finally said, sounding as if he'd been holding his breath. "I haven't had any grease since Sully moved in. The man's become a health nut. My kingdom for a cheese steak."

She chuckled but knew he was battling as hard as she was to keep things light. "You'd run five miles a day if it meant you could eat a steady diet of junk food. I'll see you at one-thirty."

It felt as if the clock moved in slow motion, but at last it was time for her to leave. Adam was already in a booth when she got to the deli. He was staring out of a window, so deep in thought that she had settled across from him before he noticed her presence. Then he just looked at her, his gaze seeming to drink in her features.

"Do I have a smudge on my nose?"

"I was just making up for lost time. I'm sorry I didn't call. I needed space."

Xandra slipped out of her coat and stacked it with her purse next to her on the seat. "Space for what?" she asked.

"To get my head together." Adam hunched over

his coffee. "I asked you out that first time because I like you. And I thought we could be friends. Keep each other company. Then, there we were, standing in the sunset, and I was kissing you. 'Friends' was suddenly a little too mild a word for what I felt. And what I felt was something I didn't think I was ready for." He paused, leaning back. "There have been women in my life over the years. Several."

He didn't sound proud of the fact, but neither did he sound as if he were confessing to plentiful indiscretions. She grinned.

"What?" he asked, his eyebrows dipping in the center as they always did when he was puzzled.

"I've heard all about your extensive love life. Several times, now that I think on it." She sent him a teasing smirk as she lifted the menu, pretending to examine it.

"What?" He frowned fully now. "How could you have heard that?"

"Mark. He thinks you're a lady-killer and about to break my heart."

Now his eyebrows rose in shock. "Mark said that? Look, I wasn't trying to be cruel. I didn't plan that kiss, and I certainly didn't expect the way it felt. I backed off to *keep* from hurting you. I needed to get my head around what was happening and to see if time away from seeing you would change anything. It didn't change a thing." He snapped the menu he'd been holding behind the napkin dispenser. "Except Sully told me he'd pitch me in the pool if I didn't shape up."

"That's quite a threat. I thought Beth had paid to have that pool drained."

Adam grimaced. "She did. Sully's not happy with me at all," he admitted before taking her hand.

Her pulse took off at a gallop, his touch no less electric than it had been.

"Ten years and no one has ever made me feel what you did when I kissed you," he told her, and traced his thumb over the back of her hand.

"And has there been any steady person among the bevy of beauties floating through your life in that last ten years?" she forced herself to ask. If Sky James was a factor, she had to know. Now. Before she let her heart become even more involved.

"No." Adam looked confused and a little worried. "Is my past some kind of a problem for you? You know, the way your divorced status was for you?"

"Not at all." She couldn't fight a grin. She didn't intend to mention Sky James—at least not yet. "Just checking my sources. So where do we go from here?" she asked, not sure where her sense of calm had come from at first, but when she thought about it, she knew. The Lord had her in the palm of His hand.

"Where?" He lifted his shoulders, but it wasn't a careless shrug. It was a gesture of acceptance. "We spend time together. See what develops."

She nodded. "Sounds like a plan."

His green eyes widened. "I don't have to grovel?"

She shook her head. "Nary a bow nor a scrape."

He took a deep breath and seemed to relax before

a wide grin spread across his face. "*Cats* is playing at the DuPont Hotel. Suppose I get tickets." He named several well-known actors and actresses who were part of the traveling cast.

She grinned. "Just let me know what night, and I'll meet you at your house. A certain source needs to learn that manipulation doesn't pay. *He* can do the bowing and scraping."

Adam nodded. "Ah, Mark. I should leave him to you, then?"

"By all means."

The unlikeliest of butlers, Sully, retired Senior Chief Sean Sullivan, opened the Boyer's door to Xandra the next night. The older man wore tan camouflage pants and a tan T-shirt, sans sleeves. A seal tattooed on his left upper arm had faded to a muted blue-gray, alluding to a long career. Sully was a perfect cross between Mr. Clean and Popeye the Sailor and, from what Adam had said, that described his personality to a tee, as well.

"Come on in, Ms. Lexington. Mark is in the games room. The commander's running late, but he suggested you might enjoy waiting in there for him."

Xandra grinned and handed Sully her jacket. She wore a silver-blue silk Yves Saint Laurent sheath she'd picked up at a Main Line thrift shop for a tiny fraction of the original cost. From the expression on Sully's face, she was sure the older man knew what was coming. She intended to confront Mark. Adam didn't deserve to have his life manipulated once again by someone he loved.

"Your boss is right. Show me the way."

He led her through the wide foyer past the staircase and down a hall that ended at a large room that ran across the back of the house. It was clearly an addition, with Palladian windows, a cathedral ceiling and beautiful hardwood floors. She could see why Adam had chosen this room.

"Ms. Lexington!" Mark gasped, jumping to his feet, forgetting about the show he'd been watching. "Hi. How come you're here?"

"Your father and I are going to a play. We decided to leave from here, but he's running late."

Mark clearly didn't know what to say beyond "Oh."

"His being late works out well, since it gives you and me time to catch up. I haven't seen you around. How are things going here at home?" Xandra asked as she settled on the sofa. It was another leather piece, distressed and masculine-looking but soft and smooth as butter. It sat in the middle of the big room facing away from the hall entrance.

Mark sank to the floor, taking up his previous position but ignoring the television. She knew from what Adam had told her that they'd very nearly reversed roles as far as testiness went. He'd admitted he'd been so grouchy that even Mark had complained.

"I ask how things are going because I understand your father's been so grumpy and out of sorts, Mr. Sullivan threatened to toss him in the pool. Since the pool's empty, I have to assume things have been pretty tense. I wonder why your dad would be so unhappy?''

''I dunno,'' Mark replied, and went back to his program. He pretended great interest. He might have pulled it off had a well-played commercial not been running at the time.

''Suppose I tell you why he's been so upset. He says he missed me. How does that make you feel? After all, you tried to stop me from seeing him. Do you still think I should do as you suggested? Because if you do—'' she pointed her thumb over her shoulder toward the front of the house ''—I have my car here. I can just leave. He may be disappointed but—''

''But Mark would have his way, and he'd have me all to himself,'' Adam said from behind her. There was a definite edge to his tone.

Xandra jumped to her feet as Mark twisted around, thunderstruck at Adam's sudden appearance. Mark had clearly never expected to face Adam with his little manipulations. She'd thought back over all Mark's references to Adam's romantic past and realized that, almost from the first, Mark had been trying to discourage her from becoming close to his father.

She pivoted to face Adam. Was this evening even more important to him than she'd hoped? She prayed it was so.

''That isn't what I want at all!'' Mark claimed. ''I want you to finally be happy, Dad. That's why I called Aunt Sky. She's trying to find a way to visit.

She'll cheer you up. I told her how you hate the house and how miserable you are now that you retired. She always makes you happy. If you and her got toge—''

The look that spread over Adam's handsome features stopped Mark in mid-word. In spite of the delicate nature of the situation, Xandra had a hard time not grinning. *Horrified* was too mild a word to describe Adam's expression.

''You think something's possible between me and *Sky?* Mark, I've know her since she was your age. She's like a little sister to me. Yeah, she makes me laugh, but so does Beth. She just isn't ever going to be more to me. Ever.''

Mark's lip curled a bit. ''And I suppose Ms. Lexington is? Then you'll get tired of her, or she'll get mad at you, and I won't have her for a friend anymore.''

Adam, clearly at a loss for a response, turned his hands palms up and looked at her. ''Ball's in your court,'' he muttered, and paced to the fireplace at the other end of the room.

''We're not running off to Vegas, Mark. We're taking in a play together because we enjoy each other's company. Neither your father nor I can predict the future. We don't yet know where our friendship is headed. But I can tell you this, I would never turn away from you because of something that did or didn't happen between your father and me. He's been alone for a long time. Do you really want me to walk out that door?''

Mark cast a quick glance at Adam. There was silence for a grueling length of time, although it was probably only a few seconds. Then a grin broke out on Mark's face. "Nah. You two kids go have fun. And don't be late. It's a school night," he said in a teasing voice three octaves deeper than his normal one.

"Okay, then," Adam said, just a bit breathlessly and obviously more than a little taken aback by Mark's quick turnaround. "Don't give Sully any grief. I'll see you in the morning."

Chapter Seventeen

Xandra flipped her calendar past the coming weekend to ready it for Monday morning. She grinned and wrote a tiny number "3" between the two ones of the eleven. Then, as an afterthought, she picked up her red pen and encircled the number with a heart. Three weeks had passed since Adam had called with that lovely edge of desperation in his tone.

After her solitary existence she felt as if the Lord had opened up her world, even possibly given her a family. She spent all her free time with Adam and Mark and even sometimes Sully. Last Sunday before evening services they'd taken advantage of the warming weather with a barbecued dinner on the stone terrace. Adam had overdone the steaks, Mark had underdone the baked potatoes, the corn on the cob tasted like the frozen variety it was, but Sully didn't have to cook, and the meal was the best she'd ever eaten.

Everything in life wasn't perfect, of course. Adam

was on what could only be called a theological quest. Unfortunately, he was trying to understand the gift of salvation with his head and not his heart. She told herself everyone had to listen for the knock of the Lord in their own way. It was frustrating, however, to watch him worry over every decision that came his way when he could experience tremendous peace were he able to put his future into God's faithful hands.

She had opened her top drawer to lock away the few files left on her desk when her gaze fell on the wedding album Michael had sent her. Michael and her shame over the way he'd treated her during their marriage was the biggest shadow on the horizon. What would happen if he showed up? And how would Adam react to her past cowardice? She still hadn't found the courage to tell Adam the full truth about the reasons for her divorce, though they had talked about the abuse she'd suffered at her brother Jason's hands. There had been a few times when she had nearly told him about Michael, but she'd retreated, convincing herself the time wasn't right.

"Xandra," her co-worker, A.J., said as he knocked on the door frame of her open door. "Someone dropped a piece of your mail in my in-box. Sorry. I didn't notice it until just now."

She stood and put her hand out. "Thanks. I'm sure it isn't important if it was from outside the building," she said, noticing the stamp in the upper right corner.

"Well, here it is, anyway. I'm heading home. Have a good weekend," A.J. told her.

"You too," she said, but the smile froze on her face as her eyes focused on the handwriting. Her heart started to thunder just knowing she was still in his thoughts.

It was Michael's.

Oh, Lord, please help me.

Adam checked his watch. Xandra was really late. And that was completely unlike her. "Mark, you're sure it was her car you just saw in the back lot?" he asked his son.

"Dad, Ms. Lexington has a white convertible. It's unique. Believe me. It's there." Mark's eyes strayed to a group of students talking under the flagpole. "Why don't you just go up and check on her? I'll find something to do."

Adam noticed Mark's gaze follow one particular female student as she moved through the crowd.

"So, *that's* the girl? She's kind of cute. I guess you'd like your old man to disappear and quit cramping your style, huh?"

Mark sent him a crooked smile. "It couldn't hurt."

"I'll go hurry Xandra along, but be ready to roll when we get back."

"Don't hurry on my account," Mark tossed over his shoulder as he slid from the car.

Adam chuckled and went after the woman he was quickly coming to see as his future. He could no longer imagine life without Xandra. Luckily, he didn't think Mark could, either. As he walked through the nearly silent halls, he thought back to his own days in that very school. He'd been Mark's age when he'd seen recruitment literature in the guidance office. It hadn't been there for students in his upper track, but that hadn't mattered to Adam. He'd altered the idea of the Navy to include Annapolis and seen freedom from the demands of his parents as well as the life he'd wanted. And now he'd come full circle. He was back walking the same halls.

The door to Xandra's office was open just as it had been the day he'd approached it for their second meeting. He stopped, standing in the same spot where he'd stood back then, trying to size her up before she noticed him. He frowned. Today, as that day, she looked upset and incredibly vulnerable. Concerned, he started forward. Today he wasn't an intruder. The woman he thought might very well be his future needed his comfort.

"Xandra, what's wrong?" he asked, not even pretending that something might not be.

She looked up at him, guilt written on her features. "I'm so sorry. I never thought it would go this far."

His heart stopped. "Us?" he asked, unable to move farther into the little airless room. He already felt as if he were choking.

"Yes." Tears coursed down her face. "No," she corrected, and shook her head hard, whipping her long straight hair across her face so that several strands stuck to her wet cheek. "I lied. All this time, I've lied. I was too much of a coward to tell you."

"What are you saying? That you never wanted me

in your life? That we shouldn't see each other anymore?" Was that raspy voice really his?

Her face crumpled. "I don't think that'll stop him now. My mother must have told him all about you. I knew you could take care of yourself, but I didn't think of Mark. I'm so sorry."

Air flowed back into his lungs. She didn't regret their relationship. Something else had her literally shaking. Adam was through the doorway and kneeling at her side in a second, smoothing the hair off her face. "She told who about us? Xandra, try to make some sense, honey. I can't fix what's wrong if I don't know what it is."

"You can't fix Michael. I don't think anyone could. And now my mother told him we're seeing each other." She held out a moist, crumpled piece of paper.

Adam took the paper from her damp hands and read.

Alexandra,
It seems forever since I last saw you, my darling, but you will always be mine—heart and soul. Know that, and that I am keeping current on your life. I was so distressed to learn you've been seeing someone your dear parents feel is unsuitable. You've become such a disappointment. Your mother told me all about him. It would be such a shame if anything happened to orphan his son. Or if the boy were to have some sort of catastrophic accident.
I'm counting the days until we're together again.
                                                Michael

Everything that had remained a mystery about Xandra from the first moment he'd met her was now crystal clear. He looked up and she turned away, shame replacing the apology in the soft gray of her eyes.

"He abused you."

It hadn't been a question, but she nodded as if it had.

"Why didn't you tell me?" he asked, pitching his voice to keep any hint of censure out of it. He was disappointed that she hadn't trusted him, but not angry. Not at her, anyway. But Balfour had better stay out of his way!

"I never thought he'd go after you or Mark," Xandra whispered as she stared down at her hands where they lay balled up in her lap.

He took her gently by her chin and got her to look at him. "I'll take care of Mark. *And* you. I meant, why didn't you tell me about what your ex-husband did to you?"

"I couldn't." She bit her lip and looked away, breaking his heart in a new way that flooded him with tender feelings for her. "I just couldn't make myself tell you. How could I tell a man who spent a major portion of his life facing untold dangers that I was such a coward I let Michael hurt and terrify me for nearly two years?"

She didn't understand what courage meant. "You left. That took courage."

She shook her head. "No. The son of our new housekeeper rescued me. He gave me clothes and a bus ticket, then he snuck me away from the vineyard. He sent me to San Diego."

That took him back a step and he grimaced with regret. "You were so close to Coronado. If only I'd known you then. Why did he choose San Diego?"

"They have a wonderful domestic abuse program. They put me in touch with an attorney named Virginia Talmadge. She filed for a protection order and forced Michael into agreeing to the divorce."

"And so you came back here to live with your parents?"

"No. At first I didn't intend to come here. When the papers were filed, I was still at one of the women's shelters in San Diego. Someone saw a man hanging around. She thought he was following me. The police got rid of him, but within a week another one showed up. It really freaked the other women and their kids. I snuck away one night. I knew my divorce was in the works, so I kept in touch with my attorney as I kept moving, heading this way, thinking my parents would help me."

She chuckled but it wasn't a happy sound, it was one of disgust. "It sounds like a soap opera. Especially when you add that I went through all that to get here and then my mother wouldn't let me stay with them. After a lifetime of having her believe Jason over me, you'd think I'd have learned. But she said helping me would only encourage me to remain separated from Michael. Then she called him as soon as I left.''

''Where did you go?''

''To Beth and New Life Inn. I walked there from my parents' house, and Beth took me in. That was a year ago last November. I still live there and help Beth run the place. I've stayed there partially because the location is secret. I've felt relatively safe and thought he'd eventually move on with his life. Now I know he knows where I work and that he hasn't moved on at all.''

Adam was so angry he felt as if his head would explode, but he refused to let Xandra see. Instead he put his hand on her shoulder. ''I don't know how you can see yourself as a coward. Balfour was the coward. I, for one, am proud of the woman you are. Your housekeeper's son might have encouraged you, helped you when you needed it. But you walked out the door, climbed into his car and onto a bus to freedom. You rescued yourself. And then you left the relative safety of that San Diego shelter to strike out on your own because Balfour's lackeys were upsetting the other residents. You came back here and built a good life for yourself. You started dating me even though your own mother was keeping tabs on you for Michael.'' Then it dawned on him. ''This was the other thing you were concerned about that day at the café.''

''I was still so afraid. Even of you. Pastor Jim helped me see that my fear of you was irrational. That was why I came to see you that day.'' She sighed. ''I knew he'd probably found out I was back here in

Pennsylvania but I'd hoped he'd just stay away, especially with the divorce final. Our dating has set him off just as I tried to warn Mother it would. She clearly didn't listen. It's his need to control me. I guess he thought he still had some power until I found someone else.''

He touched her shining hair. ''I'll have to thank him.''

''Maybe you shouldn't. Your son wouldn't be in danger if I'd just stayed away. I never thought Michael would bring either of you into this. Why aren't you angry?''

''Oh, I'm angry, Xandra. But not at you. Balfour, however had better stay on the left coast if he knows what's good for him. I'll take care of Mark. And I'll take care of you, if you'll let me.''

She straightend her shoulders, her fighting spirit returning. ''I told you I'm not afraid. Pastor Jim told me the Lord doesn't give us a spirit of fear.''

She looked as dangerous as a spitting kitten. ''Honey, I don't think he meant you should *never* be afraid. There are times when fear is a pretty bright thing to feel. I imagine Jim Dillon meant you shouldn't be afraid when you have no reason to be. But that doesn't mean Balfour isn't dangerous.''

''Believe me, I know how dangerous he is.''

The muscles in Adam's stomach knotted at the knowledge of danger and remembered pain on her face. He would not let that man hurt her again. ''The first thing I think we need to do is call the police. In my book, this is a threatening letter. Jack's brother-in-law, Jim Lovell, is a detective with the state police.

He's actually a lieutenant so he must be pretty good at what he does and I've been in his company several times with Beth and Jack. He's a nice guy. Let's go collect Mark. I'll call Jim on the way to the car. He can meet us at my house.''

She looked at her watch, only then becoming aware of how much time had passed. ''Oh! Mark isn't with you and everyone's gone. He shouldn't be alone.''

''He's with a group out front near the flagpole, but I'll feel better when he's with me or Sully. Let's roll, honey.''

On the way to the car, Adam had the mobile operator contact Jim Lovell, then they picked up Mark. When they reached Boyerton they found Jim out front leaning against a candy-apple-red 1965 Mustang. She'd met him once at Laurel Glen. A big Nordic-looking guy, he was always with his wife, Crystal, Jack Alton's sister. Today, unfortunately, he was alone and he was on duty.

Mark had taken the news in stride, though he was furious that someone had dared to hurt and frighten Xandra. Now all he wanted was permission to crawl all over Lovell's car. Jack's brother-in-law waved him on and followed them inside. Jim read the letter, and his reaction made Adam wonder if Michael Balfour knew there was a line forming for the chance to teach him a lesson.

''Not a dumb man, unfortunately,'' Lovell said. ''This is couched in terms general enough that any lawyer could argue successfully that he is just passing on concerns and hoping to save you heartache.''

''We're divorced. Doesn't that mean anything?''

Lovell leaned forward in his chair. "Look, we know what he means but we can't prove it. I'd never be able to get him extradited to face harassment or threat charges. It's what I'd like to do, but I have to operate within the law." He shrugged, clearly frustrated to have his hands tied.

"But what about Mark? Can he threaten a child and get away with it?" Xandra demanded.

Adam had to hand it to her. She wasn't cowed by Balfour popping up like this. And she was mighty angry at the threat to Mark.

"It's frustrating. We can get a protection order, but it would have to state where you live so he knows where he can't go. And I still can't touch him unless he comes near any of you. And then he'd know where the shelter is."

"That just isn't acceptable," Adam said. Maybe as a cop, Jim Lovell couldn't touch Balfour, but let him come near either Xandra or Mark…

Lovell grimaced. "I wouldn't see it as acceptable, either. A little over a year ago, I was in a similar situation. There was someone stalking Crystal before we were married. Your sister Beth was nearly killed with Crystal. My suggestion to you, Xandra, is be vigilant. Try not to go anywhere alone. Vary your routine. The same goes for Mark." He paused. "Adam, I think we can assume you can take care of yourself, but keep a close eye on your son."

Adam shot him a wry grin. "I wish he *would* come after me."

Chapter Eighteen

Xandra watched a implacable smile form on Adam's lips. He looked so utterly dangerous when he smiled that way that it was easy to forget how gentle a man he was. It didn't bode well for Michael if Adam ran across him. Anyone who knew Adam knew what was in his heart, but they also were sure he was capable of dealing with an enemy. He'd smiled at her like that at their first meeting. It had rattled her then, but it didn't now.

Now, she felt protected.

Being protected and cherished by someone was an altogether new and different feeling for her. It was a good feeling, and she sat back for a second to savor it. But good feeling or not, that didn't mean she intended to hide behind him or purposely put him in harm's way.

"Adam, I don't want him coming after any of us. Don't wish for something like that."

Adam leaned forward, his eyes darkened and grave. "I'd rather be the target than have him go after you or Mark. Maybe I'll write him. Flush him out."

"No. Please. I know you could handle yourself against him in a fair battle, but he doesn't fight fair."

Adam nodded. "I know that. Cowards and bullies never do. He's also not likely to come after me. He'll pick on someone he perceives as an easy target." He looked toward the lieutenant. "Maybe I should drive Xandra to and from the school until we know which way the wind blows with this guy."

"Go with her everywhere if you can. She shouldn't be alone," Lovell said, flipping his notebook closed.

"Absolutely not," she told them. "The location of the shelter has to remain a secret."

"I have an in with the outgoing director," Adam said, his grin still a bit wolfish, but teasing, too. "Beth'll okay my knowing the location. She can explain what's going on to the women. Honey, you can't go zooming up and down these back roads alone."

She couldn't help remembering the story Beth had once told her about the husband of one of the residents. He'd learned Beth's connection to the shelter and run her off the road. With that memory, a little of Xandra's confidence eroded.

"Besides," Adam was saying, "suppose you accidentally lead him to New Life? He's hired professionals in the past to track you. What makes this any different? Imagine how much it would shake those women to find Michael Balfour knocking on the front door. They'd never feel safe there again.''

He never ceased to amaze her with his ability to be so strong and capable and think so logically, yet but still be sensitive to the feelings of others. And he was right about everything. She huffed out a little breath. So, okay. There was little doubt it was time to give in, but she did so with a few reservations.

"If you're driving me, what about Mark?" she asked. "You realize he can't come to New Life with you. The women would worry he's too young to be trusted with that information. They'll worry enough just seeing you.''

"Mark will be Sully's territory. He can take Mark in and do a sweep of the school when they get there to make sure Balfour isn't lurking somewhere. Can you have a car drive by the school on and off through the day, Jim?"

"No problem. I think I'll go see your parents, Xandra. Advise them to back off from Balfour. That might close the pipeline of information. And with that, I guess we have a plan," Lovell said, standing. "If you hear anything else from him, let me know right away.''

Adam saw Jim Lovell out as Xandra mulled over her options. She put her feet up and closed her eyes. It wasn't easy to swallow the truth. After all she'd done to put Michael and their marriage behind her and move on, she wasn't free of him. Maybe she'd never be free. How long was she supposed to look over her shoulder? How long was Mark supposed to curtail his activities and go everywhere with a sixty-year-old baby-sitter?

She took a deep breath and started to pray. She prayed for peace and safety, for Adam and Mark in general and for the courage she'd need if forced to face Michael. She prayed her parents would finally believe her about her marriage and come to understand that money and culture didn't make Michael a good person.

Lost in her prayers, she fell into a deep dreamless sleep.

Sometime later the sweet smell of the spring breeze stirring memories of the fun they'd had on the terrace the Sunday before woke her and drew her outside. She barely heard Adam call her name sometime later.

"Out here," she replied.

"I came in to check on you and you were gone. It's gonna be okay, Xandra," he said, wrapping his arms around her waist from behind. "We'll get through this."

"I know. Thanks for the nap. I guess I needed it. That letter was just such a shock," she said, and leaned against his solid strength, borrowing just a little for herself. His scent, something woodsy with a hint of spice, enveloped her. She looked down at his muscular forearms, as always fascinated by the fine honey-colored hairs covering them.

The sun continued its slow descent as they watched the sky turn a brilliant golden pink. It occurred to her as the gilded light turned the evening to magic that she loved this tough, sensitive, and oh-so-stubborn man with all her heart.

"Do you want to go home to change for dinner?" he asked as the shadows disappeared and night began to fall. "We're going out. You, me and Mark."

She dropped her head on his shoulder. "Do you think that's wise?"

"It's what we'd planned. Mark and I had a snack to hold us until you woke. We aren't doing anything wrong in seeing each other, and I refuse to let that man dictate what I can do with my life. How about you?"

"No. You're right."

"Good. By the way, I called Beth. She's going to talk to everyone at the shelter. Sully and I will take care of getting your car over here tomorrow." He turned her in his arms and hugged her close. "It'll be okay."

She took a half-step back and looked up, caressing his smooth, recently shaved cheek before sifting his shower-damp hair through her fingers. In spite of the threat from her past, she'd never had a more beautiful moment than standing there in Adam's arms.

"I love you," she whispered, and stood on tiptoe to kiss his lips.

Adam jerked back, breaking the contact of their lips, but he held her a little tighter. His eyes had widened so much that she nearly laughed. She didn't expect him to reciprocate, though she was a bit sad for him that he couldn't. She really thought he loved her, but she understood why those words would be difficult for him. It had been only a matter of months since he'd arrived at the place where he could let go of all the love he'd felt for his ex-wife. Adam didn't love easily, but once won, his love would be the kind to last a lifetime. He opened his mouth to say something, but she silenced him with her fingertips.

"Adam, you don't need to say anything. I didn't tell you to pressure you. Love is freely given. It has no strings. And I can wait because it also is patient." She chuckled, hoping to lessen the tension that suddenly charged the air. "Goodness, I sound as if I'm rewriting Corinthians. I know the Lord's hand is on us and our relationship. It'll all be fine."

A month later, Xandra still believed that. She and Adam had grown closer in the hours and days that had followed that golden moment out of time. Proximity only increased the feelings of love for him that she had recognized that beautiful night. Adam continued on his theological quest, frequently meeting with Jim Dillon when his questions were beyond her or Mark's biblical expertise. She and Mark would shake their heads at his futile attempts to be logical about something as illogical as faith. Then they sent him to their capable pastor. Mark even sheepishly apologized to Jim Dillon for his father's stubbornness. The pastor laughed and said he enjoyed the chance to match wits with someone so intelligent. It was clear their pastor considered himself the winner.

On another front, Adam continued his sweeping renovations on the house. He pulled down the overgrown "Boyerton" sign at the head of the drive after Mark uncovered a historic stone marker naming the place "Willow Haven." Mark's discovery redefined the estate's roots for Adam, since he'd never known there had been an earlier name.

Adam and Mark held a fun-filled renaming ceremony and picnic on the first weekend in June to unveil the restored marker at the base of the drive renaming the estate Willow Haven. They celebrated with the help of an ever-widening circle of friends who were all connected to either the Taggerts and Laurel Glen or the Tabernacle.

Beth and Jack were slated to leave for Colorado toward the end of June when Jack's contract with Laurel Glen was up. They would be doubly missed— they had announced that they were expecting twins late next winter.

Thanks to Meg Taggert and her work with the Chester County Historical Society, the house would soon have a new-old look to go with the new-old name. It was now Willow Haven, as it had been in past generations. At the party, Meg presented Adam with a picture of Willow Haven's main house from earlier in the century. Everyone was pleasantly surprised by the difference a friendly, whimsical-looking porch had once made in the appearance of the dour-looking home. Reconstruction of the ornate porch that had once nearly wrapped the house was now under way.

Michael had not contacted her again. After the visit from Jim Lovell, her father called to apologize for not understanding the seriousness of the problems in her marriage. The women at New Life took Adam's comings and goings, brief and unobtrusive as they were, quite well. And Mark made plans to spend most of his summer either riding or swimming with new friends in the now restored pool.

"Have a good summer, Ms. Lexington. You too, Mark," a female student called into her office as she passed by. Xandra grinned at the girl's flirtatious tone toward Mark. As Xandra had predicted, he was the school's newest heartthrob.

Over the summer the offices were being shuffled around and painted, so, now that the last day of school had arrived, it was time to pack all her personal things for the trip home. Mark had volunteered to help and they only had that day to get it done. The workers planned to begin renovations on the second floor of the school in the morning and no one was to be allowed back in after today. In fact, they'd already begun in the basement, having somehow accidentally cut the main telephone lines that ran through the school. Consequently, the faculty was relegated to using their personal cell phones.

"Mark, would you hand me that empty box over there?" she asked as she taped up and labeled a finished one.

"Sure thing. You want the books packed in order, or doesn't it matter? I think I can get more in each box if I can shuffle them around by size, and since Dad and I will be carrying them, we can pack heavy."

"That's true. I—" Xandra's cell phone rang from

under a pile of something, drawing her attention. "Where on earth did I leave the thing now? Can you tell where it's coming from?"

Xandra and Mark looked frantically for the source of the muffled ring. They both laughed when they found the useless regular phone, then escalated into giggles as they turned the office into a genuine disaster area while the cell phone continued to elude them. Some posters she'd laid across her desk finally slid to the floor, uncovering the phone on the other side of the desk from where she stood. Xandra lunged and wound up lying across her desk on her stomach as she scooped it up and pushed the answer button.

"Hello," she said, still laughing at the slapstick scene they'd just gotten caught up in.

"Alexandra? Is that you? It's your father."

Mark laughed again as she pushed herself into a sitting position, and she swatted him on the head with a packing tube. "Sorry, Father. Mark and I are packing up my office. There's general mayhem in here right now. What can I do for you?" she asked.

"You can come over here and talk some sense into this stubborn mother of yours," her father groused.

"Mother? What makes you think she'd listen to me about anything? Actually, I'm probably the last person whose opinion she'd value."

"Ordinarily, I wouldn't bother you. Heaven knows, she hasn't been there for you. Neither of us has. But she's having chest pains and refuses to let me either call 911 or take her to the hospital."

Alarm shot through Xandra. "Chest pains?"

"She's never even hinted at a heart condition, but now I wonder if she thought I wouldn't want to deal with it. I'm worried, Alexandra," her father said, his tone grave.

"I'm sure you are. You really think she'd listen to me?"

"Actually, she said, 'Why don't you call Alexandra? You seem to value her opinion over mine lately. She'll tell you you're being hysterical and ridiculous.'"

"Oh. Not exactly a ringing endorsement."

"She's just being difficult. I'm out of options other than calling the ambulance against her wishes. You can't imagine what it would be like around here if I did that. I thought I'd call you and call her bluff in one fell swoop. Let's face it, *I* knew you wouldn't do anything but insist she be checked out."

"Are the pains moving? Is she experiencing pain anywhere else?" she asked, remembering a pamphlet she'd read on women's heart issues.

"All she says is she's in pain. We were arguing, you see. I've been trying to do more away from the office. I made plans to surprise her and take her to the country club. I came home and she was upset that I hadn't warned her. I feel so responsible. All we've done is argue for over a month, since I ordered her not to contact that miscreant you were married to."

"I'm sorry to have caused problems between you two. Have you called Dr. Avery?"

Her father sighed deeply. "Can't. He's on vacation in the south of France."

Xandra could tell her father was completely un-strung. She'd come to understand him in the last month. He hadn't abdicated his parenthood because he didn't want to be a parent. Apparently, making personal decisions had paralyzed him, since an incident in his boyhood where a wrong decision caused him great heartache.

"I don't have a car, Father," she said, guilt pricking her. Then she remembered A.J. and the over-crowded office next door to hers that he'd occupied for ten years. He'd be packing and tossing old college catalogs for hours yet. "Wait. My colleague might lend me his car. I'll be there as soon as I can. Otherwise, I'll have to wait for Adam to bring me. But I will be there."

Her fathe sighed. "Oh, bless you."

She ended the call and put down the phone as she started for the door.

"Ms. Lexington, where are you going?" Mark asked.

The concern in his voice stopped her. She took a moment to explain the situation, then ran next door and had to explain all over again, knowing the clock was ticking. A.J. was more than happy to lend her his car as long as she understood it wasn't in the best of shape. She ran back to her office moments later, keys in hand, and grabbed her purse.

"You can't go alone!" Mark declared mutinously. "She isn't worth the risk."

"Mark, I have to go now. I know you don't think much of her, but she is my mother. And Father asked for my help. He needs me. He's trying to change, and I have to be there for him. I have to go."

Xandra ran out, hearing Mark shout his objections after her, and rushed to A.J.'s little rust bucket. She all but dove behind the wheel, but there her rapid forward progress slowed to a standstill. The stubborn car refused to start. Just when she was beginning to worry she'd have to give up, the engine finally turned over.

With a sigh of relief she put the car in drive, wondering frantically, what was her mother thinking to refuse medical help? Goodness, she was on the ladies' auxiliary of two hospitals!

Mark frowned and sealed the box of books. Ms. Lexington had been so upset, she'd never answered how she wanted the books packed, so he'd decided on using more boxes and packing them in alphabetical order. Just as he finished taping the box, the cell phone on her desk rang. He hesitated but decided he'd better answer it in case it was his dad.

"Hello?" he said.

"I thought this was Alexandra Lexington's number," an older man said.

"It is, sir. I was helping her here in her office. She was so upset, I guess she left without her phone. Are you Ms. Lexington's father?"

"Yes, I am. I'd hoped to catch her. Her mother's finally agreed to go to the hospital. We're en route now. Perhaps you could catch her? Alexandra could meet us there." Mark could hear Mrs. Lexington in the background objecting to her husband's call.

"I can try to catch her. But she's been gone a while."

"Try, please," Mr. Lexington said. "I'd feel so much better having her support once we get there. Our house is in the opposite direction. It's going to take her so much longer if she gets there and finds we've left."

"Okay," Mark agreed, then couldn't resist adding, "This wasn't a good idea, you know. My dad didn't want her alone."

Mark hung up without waiting for Mr. Lexington's reply. He ran through the hall, down the steps, then up another ground-floor hall toward the teachers' parking lot. Just as he burst out the side door, Mark saw Ms. Lexington pull out onto Indian Creek Road. He stopped, frustrated, leaning his hands on his thighs to catch his breath. Then he saw a long luxury car pull away from the curb. The man behind the wheel looked an awful lot like the man his father had shown him a picture of—Michael Balfour, Ms. Lexington's ex-husband. The big car made a U-turn and followed her. It had a California license plate.

Michael Balfour came from California.

Mark tightened his hand into a fist and realized he still held the cell phone. His dad would know what to do. Fumbling with the key pad, he misdialed, then finally got it right and hit the call button for his dad's cell.

"Boyer," his dad answered in that no-nonsense military way he'd yet to lose.

"Dad, it's Mark. Ms. Lexington left the school.

She's driving Mr. Charles's car. Her mom got sick and her dad called because Mrs. Lexington wouldn't go to the hospital. So Ms. Lexington went to their house to convince her mother she needed a doctor. Ms. Lexington must have accidently left her cell phone behind, so when her dad called back to say her mother had agreed to go, I answered it. I ran down to try catching her, but she pulled out of the lot just as I got outside.''

"Calm down, son. It's okay,'' Adam said. "I'll just—''

"No, it isn't! A car followed her. A big black car with California plates, and the guy looked like her ex-husband!''

"Mark, I want you to call Jim Lovell. That way I can concentrate on driving. His number is stored in her phone's memory. Just press the six and hold it. Tell him all this and tell him I'm headed to her parents' house. Then call Sully to come get you. You did good, Mark. Try not to worry.''

Mark stared at the cell phone after his dad hung up the phone. "Try not to worry? Fat chance.''

Chapter Nineteen

Xandra drove as fast as A.J.'s rattletrap would let her. She saw the iron gates to her parents' Greco-Roman house slide open when she got to the end of the drive. Her father must have been watching for her arrival. That surprised her. He hadn't sounded capable of such calm thought.

As she drove through the gates, she remembered with weighty clarity standing on the street outside the locked gates, begging her mother for help through the intercom. And she remembered being turned away. Xandra honestly didn't know what she was doing there, but there was no time to analyze why she kept trying to reach out to Mitzy Lexington.

Resolute and knowing she faced almost certain rejection once again, Xandra zoomed up the driveway and screeched to a stop just past the front entrance. She leaped out of the car, ran up the three wide marble steps and tried the knob. It turned. Again her father's forethought surprised her. He had sounded so terribly rattled. Of course, "rattled" didn't exactly describe the cool and in control Geoffrey Lexington she'd thought she knew for years either.

Expecting either to have her father meet her at the door or to hear some sort of commotion from inside over her arrival, she was disquieted to be met by utter silence. The house was so silent she could hear the six-foot-long antique German regulator clock ticking where it hung on a wall just off the foyer. She called out but got no response.

Then it occurred to her that perhaps her father had at last convinced his stubborn wife to go to the hospital. He couldn't have called, since she'd left her cell phone on her desk.

Shrugging and much calmer knowing that her mother must be on her way to the hospital, she shook her head and moved back to the front door. Her poor father was at the hospital alone. He would be so out of his element he wouldn't know what to do. She reached for the door knob and turned, then paused, her mind racing.

Who had opened the gates?

Jerking open the door, Xandra gasped when she saw the man standing beyond it. Her worst nightmare had come to life.

"Michael. What are you doing here?" she demanded, reaching desperately for control.

"I've come for you." His tone said she was a fool if she even had to ask.

No! He was going to succeed in making her feel

stupid again! "Come for me? Go away, Michael," she snapped. "There's nothing left between us. You destroyed anything I ever felt for you,"

She started to swing the door closed, but Michael lunged and drove his shoulder into it, pushing the door inward, tearing it from her hand. Her fingers stung and she grabbed them with her other hand as she quickly backed away from him. But he followed, close enough for her to catch a whiff of his cologne, a heavy oppressive scent that turned her stomach with memories. What she'd once thought to be baby-blue eyes were every bit as hard and icy cold as she remembered.

"I never gave you permission to leave me," he said, his mouth pulled grotesquely into a sneer.

Xandra stiffened her back. She wouldn't cower. She wouldn't buckle. She was a coward no longer. Adam had called him a bully, and her advice to any student facing a bully was to stand up to him.

"I didn't need your permission. You married me. You didn't buy me. Then you destroyed the marriage. I merely had the contract voided. You tried to destroy me and all that I was, too, but you failed. You're nothing to me but a pathetic piece of my past. Now, get out, Michael. Go home to your little fiefdom and rule those poor migrant workers, because you're done ruling me."

Michael's face twisted farther, making his handsome face ugly and repulsive. "It's him, isn't it. That man your mother told me about? You can't want some washed-up soldier who has to live in his parents' home because he has nowhere else to go. Look at what you come from.''

Xandra couldn't help it. She laughed. ''Is that what my mother told you? I'm sorry to disappoint you, but your information is wrong, not that I care how much money Adam has in the bank. A bank account isn't the measure of a man, Michael. But it happens that Adam could probably buy and sell his parents. In fact, he did. Adam *bought* Willow Haven. And he wasn't just in the military. He was a lieutenant commander, and a Navy SEAL. So you see, he won't let your threats scare him. He's faced enemies far more dangerous than you.''

''Let me tell you something now, Alexandra,'' he said suddenly deadly calm. ''You're coming home with me whether you want to or not.''

Too late she remembered Adam's warning about the reality of bravery. There was danger in goading a bully. Especially when she wasn't as physically strong as he was and didn't know his rules of engagement. There was something more than anger in Michael's eyes. There was purpose. And no one else knew she was in danger.

He reached for her.

Xandra screamed ''No!'' Then she ran.

Adam took the turn onto Ithan Creek Road on two wheels. He jerked the wheel left and the SUV fell back onto all four. His heart pounding, he told himself that if he drove too aggressively he'd have an accident and never reach her in time.

"Please, God. Keep her safe. She's so important to me. I never thought I could feel like this. Please. I can't believe You'd bring her into my life to love and make me so happy, only to let me lose her."

Adam felt his head go just a little light for a split second. He got it. Everything Xandra had said about putting his life in God's hands made perfect sense. It was as if blinders had been on his eyes and now they were gone. His heartbeat slowed, and calm descended on him. It was going to be fine. He knew it with a certainty that was mind boggling.

"Okay, Lord. I get it. Mark's life. Xandra's life. My life. They're all in your hands. I can't see the future, so I can't plan for it in every detail. But You can. I give up. I just can't do this on my own anymore. Be my Lord. My partner. Guide my life. Please take care of her till I get there. I promise I'm going to tell her I love her, first thing."

Adam drove fast but with every needed restraint until he saw the address numbers on the white stucco pillar at the foot of the drive to the Lexingtons' luxurious gated home. The ornate wrought-iron gates at the entrance of the long drive were closed. The entire house appeared to be surrounded by an eight-foot-high iron fence topped in potentially deadly spikes. He threw open the car door and jumped out, but when he got to the gates he found them locked.

Beyond, up near the house, he could see a rusty red car he had to assume belonged to A.J. Charles. And halfway up the quarter-mile-long drive, between the gates and the house, sat the long black car Mark

had described right down to its California plates.
There was no question, Xandra was in there with her
ex-husband.

And then he heard her scream.

Xandra heard her own scream bounce off the marble walls and floor. It echoed in her mind, heightening
her fear. She ran toward the door. Michael lunged,
caught her by the hair and dragged her to the floor
with him. She pushed him away and scrambled to her
feet. Half crawling, half running, she struggled to the
front door. She'd just begun to pull it open when his
arm shot forward over her shoulder and slammed it
shut.

She whirled away, but he grabbed her hair again.
More determined than ever that this time he wouldn't
defeat her, she fought, but nothing she did seemed to
loosen his hold on her hair. Then he got one of his
hands past her defenses and grasped her by the throat.
He pushed her back against the wall and in the next
millisecond, his second hand joined the first. He
shoved his thumbs under her jaw, forcing her to look
at him. It was humiliating to be so in his power, but
she glared at him, refusing to be cowed.

His eyes held the hatred that had so shocked her
the first time she'd seen it. What had she ever done
but fall in love with him? Maybe that had been the
problem all along. She'd loved a man that had never
existed—and he'd known it. "Let me go, Michael,"
she ordered, refusing to show fear, trying to treat him

like any other schoolyard bully. "This isn't going to change anything."

He shook his head wildly. "Shut up! You made me the laughingstock of Summit Falls. I know what they're saying now. 'With all the Balfour money, *Mikey* still couldn't keep a wife. He hasn't changed a bit. He's still a loser. A runty, little loser just like back in school.' *Mikey!* One of them called me *Mikey*. Do you remember how much I hate being called that?"

Xandra could see that facing him down wasn't helping. She decided to humor him. "Yes, I remember. But I never called you that."

His eyes narrowed. "You were clever. Right to the end, you were so clever. I never saw how little you respected me. Then you ran off and I knew."

"I had to leave. You left me no choice, Michael. Can't you see that?" Xandra began to feel dizzy and thought perhaps his fingers had cut off some of the blood supply to her brain. She tried to push him away but he tightened his hold on her neck. The dizziness grew, though she could breathe just fine.

"They respected me until you," he droned on as if she hadn't spoken or struggled to get free. "I have to bring you back to show them you're still mine."

She tried to fight the leaden feeling dragging at her limbs, knowing if she passed out, he could take her anywhere without worry of her struggling. But no matter how hard she fought him and the approaching darkness, it rolled over her, engulfing her in an overwhelming weakness. She remembered to pray for help just as lights exploded like fireworks behind her eyes.

It took Adam only seconds to scale the iron gates. And he set a personal record at a full run to get to the front door. When he was about to give the door a good hard kick in the vicinity of the lock, he realized it hung open. He kicked it anyway and the door burst inward, hitting the wall. He followed in the wake of the sound, which crackled like an explosion through the foyer.

The next seconds were reflex. He grabbed the guy who had Xandra by the throat, spun him around and caught him with a good solid uppercut. Balfour dropped like a rock, and didn't move.

He turned back to find Xandra in a still, crumpled heap on the hard marble floor. He dropped to her side, his heart scarcely beating in his chest, his mind screaming desperate prayers as he rolled her over into his arms. Supporting her back with his forearm he cradled her against his chest. She was alive! He'd made it just as the Lord had made him feel he would. He'd been on time, but he'd never been as terrified in his life as when he'd seen Balfour with his hands around her throat.

He checked her pulse. It was strong and steady. "Xandra, love. Open your eyes. You're safe," he said, surprised by the raw sound of his own voice. Then a tear he hadn't realized he'd shed dropped onto her cheek, and her eyelids fluttered.

Joy burst through him. He forced himself to look

past the beauty of her soft blue eyes; the pupils looked even and responded quickly to the light pouring in the open front door, but there was confusion there as well. Frowning, she raised a shaky hand to his cheek. When it came away wet she drew her eyebrows together as if she was trying to think but with difficulty. Then he saw reality dawn in her eyes. She teared up.

"Michael was here."

"It's okay. I handled him."

"How did you know?"

"Mark saw him follow you. Mark's with Sully. Now shh, shh." Adam stared down at her, tenderness and love overwhelming him, and he dipped his head to kiss her. Breaking the kiss a moment later, he caressed her cheek. "Okay now?" he asked, his voice still rough with emotion.

She made a face. "Actually, the floor's kind of hard."

Her eyes were a little unfocused, but her look was more dreamy than confused. Exactly the way he felt every time they kissed.

"Think you can stand?"

She gave him a brave little smile. "Help me up and we'll see."

Before he could, a groan from behind Adam wiped away any lighthearted thoughts along with his smile. He looked toward Balfour and felt his gut tighten. This animal had put his hands on Xandra. He'd terrorized her for two years and now he'd crawled back to do it again. He wouldn't be showing up again. Adam intended to see to it.

Resolute, Adam helped her to her feet. Once he got her tucked somewhere safe, he and Balfour were going to have a long hard talk. By the time Xandra's ex-husband made it back to California, he was going to understand the meaning of living in fear.

Xandra lay her hand on his chest. "Don't. He isn't worth you facing an assault and battery charge."

Adam put his hands up in a hands-off gesture. "I won't touch him, but he won't know that. When I'm through with him, I'm betting he'll keep the entire country between himself and you," he promised.

A memory surfaced. One he really wished he didn't have. It was of Xandra on the way back from Maryland with her back pressed against the car door, clearly wary of him and his anger. Balfour had taught her that fear. Maybe Adam wouldn't stash her after all.

He grinned and asked, "Want to watch?"

She shrugged and looked a little unsure, but she didn't move. Balfour started to push himself onto his knees then, and Adam put his foot on the prone man's back and shoved him back down.

"Not so fast, little man. We're going to have a talk, you and I."

"You can't kill me! You'll get caught!"

Adam could feel his grin widen of its own accord. Oh, that was just too pretty a line to pass up. "Of course I can," he quipped.

"Please. Please. I'll go away and leave her alone. I'll never see her again."

"Too late. You already put your hands on her. Nobody knows you're here, so I can do what I like. The gates are locked. There's nobody to stop me. How's it feel to be powerless?''

"Her mother knows I'm here. She helped arrange the whole thing. If I disappear, she'll know," he whined.

Xandra's agonized gasp had Adam pushing down on Balfour's back with his heel just a little harder. Police sirens shrieked in the distance, growing closer by the second.

"Honey, can you open the gate for the police?"

She sniffled. "Only if they haven't changed the codes. I'll try." She turned and walked across the wide foyer to the keypad, her emotions clearly at a low ebb. Her mother had once again betrayed her, and maybe her father had been in on it, too!

Still pondering how Xandra had gotten in without the code and how the gates had gotten locked behind her, Adam knelt down next to her ex-husband. In a quiet but deadly voice that Xandra couldn't hear he said, "Here's how this is going to go. You're going to jail. Throw up any defense you want in court, but let's get this straight right now—you're safer in prison than you will be anywhere I can find you."

Adam grabbed him by the shirt and turned him so he could stick his face inches from Balfour's. "And in case you don't know, I've been trained to slip into a hostile country, take out a target and get back out with no one but the victim knowing I was there. Your tax dollars at work. So you see, coming after you will be child's play."

His hand still holding Balfour by the shirt, Adam yanked him to a sitting position and then to his feet, so he could get him handed over to the cops and away from Xandra. But Adam wasn't finished replacing bravado with fear in the small man's heart and mind. "Oh, and if, by some miracle, you beat the rap for this, don't forget to look over your shoulder from the minute you step out of the police station, because you'll never know when I'm going to show up."

A car zoomed up the driveway and Adam recognized the distinctive sound of the old V-8 engine in Jim Lovell's Mustang, so he dragged his chastened prisoner across the foyer. When Balfour turned his head to look at Xandra, Adam jerked him around and snapped, "Don't you dare even look at her."

Once out on the steps, with Lovell approaching, Adam continued with his empty threats. "We still have one more thing to talk about. If you do go to prison, and you probably will, I might get involved in living my happy life with that woman you tried to destroy, and I might forget all about you. If you're real lucky. But if I suddenly have a reason to remember you, like I hear your name when you're released sometime down the line, or you try to write her, or you hurt her or my son in any way, know that your days will be numbered in the single digits. Got it?"

The man had lost all color by then. He stammered, "Y-yes. Yes. I'll forget she ever existed. She's not worth it."

Adam narrowed his eyes. "That's where you're wrong. She's worth a hundred of you. And her con-

tinued health and happiness are worth your life,
buddy boy, and don't you forget it.''

"So is this our letter writer?" Jim Lovell asked as
he walked to meet them, whipping out a pair of shiny
handcuffs.

"He graduated. He had his hands around her throat
when I got here."

"Oh. Attempted murder, huh," Jim said.

"I was just trying to make her listen," Balfour
claimed as Jim slapped the first cuff around the Cal-
ifornian's wrist.

"Trying to make her listen? She was uncon-
scious," Adam snapped as he helped to twist Balfour's other arm back to meet the already cuffed one.
"In fact, I'd like to get back inside to her," he said
to Lovell. "By the way. Her mother set this up. Stupid woman!"

"You got that right," Jim Lovell said. "I'll be in
to take Xandra's statement as soon as a squad car gets
here to haul our problem child off to the station
house. You know, I'm tempted to charge her mother
as an accessory."

"Be my guest," Adam said, then turned away to
go offer comfort to the woman he loved.

Chapter Twenty

After Adam shoved Michael out the door, Xandra wandered into her parents' elegant parlor and sank onto the white leather sofa. The room wasn't the sort to soothe the spirit. Her mother had been after a modern minimalist look and she'd achieved it, but the iciness of her personality had come through in all the hard edges and cold steel and glass. It was elegant, but harsh and jarring.

She looked up a few minutes later as Adam's soft foot treads drew her attention. He glanced around as he entered the room, and grinned.

"And you and Mark called our house a mausoleum. Is that sofa made of marble, too?"

She shook her head. "Mother got into minimalist decorating when they traveled to Japan." Xandra smiled sadly, not ready for jokes. "Did Michael say if my father helped set me up too?"

"He only mentioned your mother," Adam answered, making his way over to sink onto the sofa next to her.

Then he did the one thing she needed most. He opened his arms to her. She fell against his hard chest as he enfolded her in the security of his embrace.

Leaning back, he took her weight and said, "I'm so sorry, honey."

"How could my father not be involved? The front door was open. They never do that. And someone opened those gates."

"The gates were locked when I got here. I thought you knew the code. I had to climb over."

Not an easy task considering the wicked-looking spikes on the top. Xandra lifted her head and looked up at Adam, feeling happiness bloom inside her in spite of what her parents had or hadn't done. She smiled. "My hero. You just need a white horse."

He kissed her on the forehead. "I'm not a hero, honey. I was just a guy afraid for my girl. You are my girl, aren't you?"

"Is that what you want?"

"I want a lot more—"

"Guess what I found in bad boy's car," Jim Lovell asked as he walked into the sunken living room. "Oops, sorry. I didn't mean to interrupt."

Adam sighed and sat up. "We'll just pick up where we left off after all this is cleared up." He gave her a look that said she could count on it.

"What is the meaning of this?" her mother's strident voice and high-heeled shoes echoed from the foyer. Then she barreled in, looking in the pink of health. "Alexandra, how dare you bring strangers into my house! And what is *he* doing here?" she demanded, pointing at Adam.

Adam took his arm from around Xandra but picked up her hand and kissed it, clearly not intimidated a whit by the infamous Mitzy Lexington on a tear. He didn't say a word. He just stared at her, his lips pursed in an angry line. The man radiated hostility. There was also a change in the affable Jim Lovell's demeanor. He'd instantly transformed into a very stern Lieutenant Lovell, State Police Detective.

"You're just in time to join the discussion," Lovell said, turning to her mother.

"I want you out of this house, sir."

"It doesn't matter what you want, ma'am, this house is now a crime scene."

Defiant, her mother arched a professionally shaped eyebrow. "Have we been robbed? Everything looks just as it should."

"Then maybe you ought to take a look at your daughter's bruised throat," Adam suggested.

"Alexandra!" her father shouted as he hurried into the room. "The officer out front told me what happened. How on earth did Michael get in here?"

"I opened the door and he was standing there," Xandra said, almost afraid to hope her father hadn't been a part of Michael and her mother's little conspiracy.

"Come in, Mr. Lexington," Lieutenant Lovell said. "You're just in time. I was about to ask a related question. One I'm sure we'll all have a great interest in getting an answer to. Please be seated.''

Her father sat. Her mother crossed her arms and stood stubbornly where she was.

"Mrs. Lexington, we could always do this in an interrogation room," the lieutenant snapped.

Her mother sat. "Fine, but I don't like your tone."

He ignored her. "Suppose you tell me what happened, Xandra. And what you can remember him saying," he added as he took out his notebook.

Xandra was surprised by how quickly she could tell the tale and how easy it was to do with Adam holding her hand. Then Adam told what had happened from his point of view.

"Okay, now that we have what happened established, I have a question to ask both of you," he said, directing his comment to her parents.

"When I came here in May, I warned you both that her ex-husband was dangerous and had sent a threatening note. I wonder if either of you would care to explain this?" He bent next to his chair and picked up a plastic bag with a remote control inside. "I tried it. It's a remote control to your front gates. It was on Michael Balfour's front seat."

"Mitzy Lexington, what did you *do?*" her father demanded, his face taking on a dull red flush.

The lieutenant shook his head, clearly disgusted. "Before your wife answers that, I'm thinking that in view of the impending charge of assault and battery and attempted murder against her former son-in-law, I should read your wife her rights."

Xandra stared in shock. "Jim, I don't want my mother arrested," she rushed to say.

Lieutenant Lovell nodded. "I'll take that under advisement. Along with what I hear. *If* Mrs. Lexington wants to waive her rights."

"She does, Detective," her father said.

"I'm not sure, Geoffrey," her mother replied.

Her father glared. "That wasn't a request, Mitzy. Answer the detective."

Mitzy blinked, clearly not used to being told what to do by anyone. "I gave the gate remote to Michael earlier and left the door opened so they'd have a private place to talk. He just wanted to talk. He said he missed her."

"And the chest pain? That was all an act to get me away from here?" Geoffrey Lexington asked. "What was the original plan before I came home unexpectedly?"

Her mother shifted nervously in her chair. "I was supposed to call her and ask her to come over. I thought I'd offer her some of my mother's jewelry, but then you came home, Geoff. I had to think of something."

Adam sat forward. "You didn't think he was dangerous? After Jim showed you that letter? What, you thought he was such a nice guy he was worried about my health and that my kid might be accident-prone? Look at what he did to your daughter."

She glanced Xandra's way, dropping her gaze to the bruises Michael had left behind, and shook her head. "I don't understand. He's from such a good family, and he always seemed like such a gentleman.''

"What's that got to do with anything?" Adam's voice rose. "That *gentleman* had his hands around your daughter's throat. Xandra told you he was dangerous. The detective told you."

"But—"

"But nothing, Mitzy," Geoffrey cut in.

Jim Lovell stood. "I think I have all I need. At your daughter's request, you won't be charged with anything. Unfortunately, I can't arrest people for being stupid. If I did, the jails would be full. I hope you realize how close you came to being charged with criminal conspiracy, not to mention almost losing your daughter." He looked at Xandra and Adam. "I'll need you each to come to the barracks to sign your statements when they've been processed. Xandra, do you need to go to the ER?"

"I'm fine. I think he'd unintentionally cut off the blood flow to my head. I really don't think he was trying to kill me. As I said, he seemed to want me to go home with him."

"I'm still charging him with attempted murder. That way I can try to force a plea bargain to the assault charge and save you from a trial, but he'll still do time. Xandra, I'm afraid I'll still need photos of your injuries as evidence."

Xandra nodded. She'd forgotten they'd need that. Another humiliating experience, thanks to Michael.

Adam sat back and put his arm around her, pulling

her close to his side. "I'm sorry, honey," he whispered, and gave Jim Lovell a salute goodbye.

Adam held Xandra, knowing full well that Jim's departure didn't signal an end to the confrontations. He intended to ask Xandra to consider marriage to him. Maybe soon, maybe sometime in the future. He had no idea if she was ready for a step like that considering how badly her last marriage had turned out for her. But he still needed her to know how he felt, and that he'd wait till she was ready.

With that in mind, there were family issues to be worked out. Namely, ancient history of the Capulet and Montague variety. He couldn't let their lives or Mark's become a battleground for real and imagined offenses. And he got the perfect opportunity the second the front door closed behind Jim Lovell.

"I suppose this is going to be in the paper," Mitzy Lexington complained.

"Is that all you care about?" Xandra asked.

"Of course not. I never meant for any of this to happen. You have to know that."

"No. I don't know that, Mother. That day I came here, running from him, you turned me away from those gates. I had to walk to the New Life Inn. Ten miles, Mother. In a denim jacket in November."

"Wait a minute," her father said, confusion infusing his voice. "Xandra, you came here first?" He glared at his wife. "And you turned her away? You told me she was living in a women's shelter as a ploy to embarrass Michael into coughing up more alimony.''

''Mother!'' Xandra turned to Mitzy, her eyes wide with shock. ''Is that what Michael told you? And you believed him? Don't you know me at all? I walked away from that marriage with the only thing I wanted—my freedom. I begged you for help and you took Michael's side over mine. You believed him, not your own daughter. Just like you did my whole life whenever I told you Jason had hurt me.''

Her mother's frown became more pronounced. ''Let us not get into your sibling rivalry with your poor, deceased brother,'' Mitzy said, her nose in the air.

''There was no rivalry. There was *fear!* My poor, deceased brother was a *monster.* Quite frankly, I thank God he died when he did.''

''Alexandra!'' both Xandra's parents gasped at once.

Adam was a little surprised himself. His gutsy gal was more than ready to wield the Montagues' sword for them, Adam thought with pride, but he was still taken aback. It seemed such a harsh thing to hear from Xandra.

''Do you want to know why I say that?'' she asked her parents. ''After all, he was out of my life where he couldn't torture and abuse me anymore. Father?''

Her mother started to stand, but her father nodded, a resigned expression on his face, and put his hand on his wife's and nodded at the chair. ''Maybe it's time we listened to our daughter and put aside preconceived notions. You convinced me she was making the same kind of false accusations against Michael that she'd made against Jason her whole life.''

''Well, that was Michael's theory,'' Mitzy replied.

Her father's frown deepened. ''Maybe she wasn't accident-prone as a child. Maybe we shouldn't have believed Jason, either.''

''Very well,'' Mitzy said, her lips in a pinched line.

With an expression like that, Adam had to wonder if she'd really listen.

Xandra took a deep breath. ''Okay. Beth didn't lie. Jason flattered her, lured her away from the school and raped her. Cole Taggert had seen them from his classroom and was suspicious because he knew Jason's reputation. Cole followed as soon as class was out, but he didn't get there in time to stop the rape.

''You've both always contended that Jason was too smart to rape a girl who could easily tell the world what he'd done. Except that Beth was never supposed to be able to tell anyone. Jason fully intended to kill her. He had the knife stabbed into the dirt next to Beth's face the whole time.''

''No. No! That can't be,'' her mother cried. ''Not my Jason.''

''Why not?'' Adam interjected, unable to keep silent a second longer. ''You were blind to your son-in-law's true nature. Why can't you be just as wrong about the past as you were about the present?''

Mitzy pursed her lips. ''I refuse to believe it.''

''*Think,* will you, Mitzy?'' Geoffrey said. ''You have to stop going through life deciding things are one way when the truth is they're another. You almost got our daughter killed. It ends here.''

Xandra stood, so Adam followed suit.

''You can go on pretending life is the way you want it, Mother,'' she said. ''Or you can face the truth. But here's the way my life is going to go from here on. I love this man. I intend to marry him one day. Adam, Mark, Elizabeth and Jack and their children, and all the children Adam and I have, will be my family. You're welcome to be a part of that family and that future, or you can leave me and mine alone. ''I've given you a lot to think about. So think. But right now, I'm leaving. Mark must be frantic.''

She turned and stalked out. Adam followed. She'd descended the steps when she stopped and turned slowly.

Her gaze rose to his and, as it did, so did the color in her cheeks. ''I can't believe I said all that.''

''She deserved it.'' He smirked, knowing she meant what she'd said about the two of them.

''I mean about *us!* I'm sorry. I can't believe I let her make me so angry. Just ignore everything I said about us.''

''Everything?'' Adam pretended disappointment and sat down on the top marble step. With her standing three steps lower, she was just about eye level with him.

''No, not everything. I love you. Of course you shouldn't disregard that.''

''You mean, you didn't mean it? You're going to renege and not marry me? I admit being proposed to in front of the bride's family was a little odd, but I thought it would be a great story to tell Mark and all those children you were talking about.''

When all she did was stare at him, her mouth slightly agape, he couldn't hold the dejected expression any longer and grinned.

She crossed her arms, trying and failing to look stern, and then she grinned too. "I said *children.* I don't remember mentioning a number that translates to *all.*''

Adam reached out. She took his hand, and he pulled until she stood on the first step, between his knees. He looked at her standing there with the breeze stirring her hair and her eyes sparkling with happiness and wanted to give her the world.

"I love you," he said, confident she'd like that gift better. "Driving here I suddenly saw that. I also got the salvation message all of you have been trying to show me. I can't describe how it felt to realize every decision didn't have to be mine alone. That He was in control so I didn't have to worry about making the right decisions if I let Him guide me."

She looped her arms around his neck. "I'm so happy for you. I know what that feeling is like and I'm sorry your moment was in the middle of a crisis."

"Don't be, honey. I never needed God more than I did on that drive over here."

"So, are going to hold me to everything I said in front of my parents?"

He kissed her, unable to wipe the smile off his face to get up even a decent pucker. "Absolutely. And I'll even cut you a break on the *all* part of the kids. We'll leave the number open to negotiation.''

"Where have you two been?" Mark shouted as he marched up the drive. "Do you know how worried I've been?"

"We," Sully added. "How worried *we've* been. And do you know how hard it is to find houses around here? How many Ithan Creek roads does one community need? Upper Ithan Creek—"

"Lower Ithan Creek. South Ithan Creek," Mark added.

"And don't forget plain old vanilla Ithan Creek that doglegs all over creation," Sully groused. "And another thing—"

"Hey, you two," Adam interrupted, now that they were nearing the steps. Clearly the only way to shut the two of them up was to stun them. Xandra might make him pay for the rest of their lives, but it'd be worth it.

"Guess what? Xandra just proposed."

Mark grinned and looped his arm around Sully's shoulders. "A take-charge woman. Exactly what this family needed."

* * * * *

Look for the next book in
the Laurel Glen Series,
AUTUMN PROMISES
in August 2004.

Dear Reader,

The characters in this book came to me slowly as the LAUREL GLEN series unfolded. It soon became apparent that the long-lost brother of a wounded girl and the sister of the guilty party had to meet. They had a million reasons to hate and distrust each other—and a million and one to fall in love. Courage and love can be born in anyone, and Jesus will save all who answer His call. This is a story that examines courage and the perceptions we have of what it means to be brave.

I've also dealt with divorce in this book and did so with a great deal of thought, prayer and research. It is a subject that often divides the church—rightly and wrongly. Divorce is a step that should never be taken lightly, and as Pastor Jim points out, should be examined on a case-by-case basis. But the truth is that only three people know if so drastic a step is justified—those directly involved and the Lord. I will always believe that it is incumbent upon the body of Christ to leave judgment to God and treat one another in love. There is an old saying that we should not judge others until we have walked a mile in their shoes. Since we mortals can never do that, perhaps we should just leave all such judgments to the Lord.

In August 2004, LAUREL GLEN will be back with the much anticipated match of Meg Taggert and Evan Alton, the man who raised her child. These two stubborn people will learn that they can find common ground and love at long last. Watch for the fireworks these two create!

God bless,

Kate Welsh

Love Inspired®

AMONG THE TULIPS

BY

CHERYL WOLVERTON

Being rescued by a celebrity wasn't something Annie Hooper was expecting while on vacation in Amsterdam. Yet she couldn't turn down handsome Victor Richardson's offer—to recover from her injuries in his château. Perhaps the lovely single mom will be given the power to heal Victor's wounded heart.

Don't miss

AMONG THE TULIPS

on sale June 2004

Available at your favorite retail outlet.

Love Inspired®

A TIME TO REMEMBER

BY

LOIS RICHER

Grayson McGonigle's world had fallen apart the day his wife and son vanished. But five months later, a traumatized Marissa and Cody reappear, unable to speak about their harrowing ordeal. Can Gray help Marissa regain her memories of their happy married life...and build a love she can never forget?

Don't miss
A TIME TO REMEMBER
on sale June 2004

Available at your favorite retail outlet.

LOVE COMES HOME

BY

TERRI REED

Rachel Maguire had always been sure of God's plan for her—a career in medicine to improve hospital conditions. That meant giving up the only man she'd ever loved: Joshua Taylor. But twelve years after she'd turned down his proposal, he was back in her life, making her wonder: Did God's plan for her include Josh and his young son?

Don't miss

LOVE COMES HOME

on sale June 2004

Available at your favorite retail outlet.

www.SteepleHill.com